Chasing Release

Five Erotic Short Stories

by

Hannah Blackbird

This is a work of fiction.
Any similarity to people, living or dead, places or events is entirely coincidental. Names, places, characters and incidents are a product of the author's imagination and are used fictionally.

This is adult reading material
Please note this book is intended for adult readership and may contain explicitly sexual themes including lesbianism, submission, voyeurism, exhibitionism, and other forms of sexual variation. Do not read this book if you find such themes offensive. None of the characters depicted in this book are related by blood

All characters in this book are adults over 18 years of age and not related

Chasing Release
Five Erotic Short Stories

Written by Hannah Blackbird
Copyright Hannah Blackbird 2018©
Published by Jim Masters
No part of this publication may be used, copied or stored in any way without the author's written permission
All rights reserved
Cover design and interior by Jake Canva

To keep up to date with the work of Hannah Blackbird promotions and free books sign up for her newsletter

www.jimmasters.co.uk
info@jimmasters.co.uk

This Collection includes the following

Chasing Release is an exciting collection of short erotic stories written by the new young author Hannah Blackbird.

Each story is complete and free-standing. Each has a fast moving story-line and twists and turns that, coupled with the well crafted erotica will have you wanting more. These stories are best read alone, anywhere but in a private place: or with your favourite person with low lights and perfumed candles.

Blown Out

The End Of Nothing

Lost Angels

Made In London

Unfamiliar

Read and enjoy. And please tell your friends about Hannah Blackbird. And watch out for more stories erotic.

Blown Out

It was dark by the time Violet made it to the car. Just another Friday evening. She'd already said goodnight to her father. He hadn't seemed to suspect a thing. Didn't he see it? Didn't he hear the mad, racing beat of her heart? It felt like a newly caged bird, trying to burst its way out of her chest. Thump. Thump. Thump. Did he know? It felt as though the world revolved around her deceit. *just another Friday evening.*

"What is it tonight?" he'd asked. He always asked but of course, she read too far into it and felt like he already suspected something.

"Just the orchestra," Her voice sounded strange and she tried to set it right. "They're doing Mozart and then Stravinsky's *Rite of Spring*. I love that piece." She'd looked up the program online, of course, feeling like a criminal the whole time. "It might go on until late," she added.

"I don't know how you can stand it," he'd yawned as she walked with a forced casualness from the room. Her shoes clicked along the hard floors, the sound interspersed by the occasional heavy rug. Ralph was at the door. They didn't speak until after he'd closed the car door behind her and was in the driver's seat.

Then he sighed.

"It'd be pointless to tell you how crazy this is, wouldn't it?" he said. He was watching her in the rear-view mirror. Violet couldn't meet his eyes.

"I'm not asking you to do anything," she said. "I just know you're too smart to get around. And I'd rather have you know about it than chase me."

"I don't really know if I should take that as a compliment," Ralph mused. He tapped out a beat on the steering wheel and went into his pocket for chewing gum, his eyes still focused on her. "Vi, I can't afford to lose this job."

"I know." She met his gaze then. "I know. And I wouldn't let that happen. Just do this one thing. Please?"

He didn't say anything.

"How's Roma, anyway?" Violet surprised herself by remembering his girlfriend's name. "Weren't you going to propose?"

Ralph blew out a sigh.

"I plan to. Just – finding a moment."

"Must be nice," Vi said. "Not needing permission to be in love."

Ralph snorted. "Must be nice living a life of obscene luxury."

"Prison is prison," Violet said. "Doesn't matter if it looks nice on the outside."

Ralph groaned.

"Fine! Enough with the theatrics! See this, kid. I won't stop you but you get caught, it's all you, okay?" He twisted in his seat to look at her, his blue eyes shaded with concern. "Vi, I don't want to see you hurt. Bottom line. You understand? You're playing with fire. You do know that, right?"

She knew it. But fire was pretty to look at and it warmed her in the most addictive way. She hadn't felt this way since – no. She frowned and tried to expel the thought. *Don't go there.*

"Vi!" Ralph was still looking at her. "I'm talking third-degree burns if you get caught. Is he really worth it?"

She bit her lip and looked down at her hands. They shook a little and she sat on them.

"Yes. I'm sorry but yes," She looked up as Zed approached the car. "He's – everything."

***

Life was routines; doing the right things, meeting the right people, perfecting the right smiles and wearing the right dresses. Nothing more. She shouldn't have even wanted more. Her life was something programmed into her, instilled since childhood and she should have accepted it. Not survived, but thrived.

But she couldn't. Too many books. As soon as she could read, she'd raced her way through every book she'd been able to find and they'd filled her head with the idea of a life that meant more. Fiction. It gave her ideas about things she should be doing. She didn't even know how other people lived, what life was like beyond her own. Nobody ever told her. The staff laughed off her questions as though she were being purposefully stupid.

And then there was Zed.

He turned up at the start of summer, a tour guide at the palace to begin with and then a minor member of the security patrol team. They crossed paths often enough to become familiar with one another and he had the kind of smile which invited conversation. It helped that he was young, maybe a couple of years older than her. He seemed amused by her almost obsessive interest in his everyday life but he humoured her all the same and she ran with it until she felt free enough to ask him anything she wanted.

Where did you grow up? Tell me about your school, your siblings, your house. Did you have to share a bedroom? What kind of food did you eat? Did you wash your own plate? How many friends do you have? How long have you known them? How many girlfriends have you had? Where do you buy food? Clothes? What do you do when your money runs out? What time do you wake, eat, sleep? What do your parents do? Do they still work? What do you do for fun?

The wrong question.

He was leaning against a statue in the sprawling flower garden, looking down at her bent over a sketchpad.

"Fun? Uh – I dunno. Go out. Drink. Maybe football. Photography."

"Oh, you're a photographer?" She looked up at him.

"Uh-huh," He looked faintly pleased with himself as though sparking her interest was an achievement. "Amateur, really. Hey, maybe I can practice on you."

Violet frowned down at her sketch more to avoid the half-proposal than anything. She'd been working on a still-life of the statue for days even though she'd never been artistically inclined. Endless lines of grey pencil spanned the page. Grey lines. Grey days.

"Violet?"

Zed was looking at her.

"I don't think so," she said apologetically. "Besides, I kind of avoid being photographed unless it's official. Can you imagine an unflattering shot on the cover of a tabloid?"

"It'd only be between us," Zed frowned. "What, you don't trust me?"

She frowned harder at her sketch, still avoiding his gaze.

"Of course I trust you. It's just – well, my dad wouldn't like it for a start."

"So don't tell him," Zed said.

She tried not to smile.

"It's really not that easy. This place is full of people. Walls have ears."

There was a pause as he digested her words.

"So we'll keep it on the quiet," he said finally, "Unless these walls have eyes too?"

"I'm serious," she laughed, looking up. "Everyone's always watching."

"We'll find a place," he said, like it was that simple. "Besides, I'm pretty crap at portraits anyway. They say the best way to improve is practice and we both have time so you'd really be doing me a huge favour."

They looked at each other. She wanted to hate him. To refuse now would seem like she was haughtily denying him something trivial. But to say yes would be to add another layer of inappropriateness to their already over-familiar relationship. She felt dangerously close to him and it had been what – a fortnight since they'd met?
"I'm not even photogenic," she stalled. "Really. I'm a terrible model. You should ask someone else."

"I don't want to ask anybody else," he replied quietly. His eyes were on hers and in the sunlight, his irises were liquid gold. Violet tucked a strand of dark hair behind her ear. The sun beat down ominously.

"Fine," she said. "But don't blame me when you end up disappointed."

He took a step closer to her.

"I won't be,"

She frowned up at him and something in his eyes darkened. His hand came out hesitantly as his tongue wet his lips. Violet could only imagine what they'd feel like against hers. She caught his wrist just before his thumb brushed her mouth.

"Not here," she said and his eyes smiled at the implied meaning.

***

There were at least a hundred people in the palace at any one time but Violet had listlessly wandered the gaping fortress for almost two decades. She knew the hidden rooms and intricate corridors like nobody else. There were always places. Places tucked away and forgotten over the seasons, locked doors and half-refurbished quarters. The top floor was a safe bet, as was the basement. The two extremes.

The attic was dusty and dry and the deeper she went, the hotter it felt. She told herself it'd be worth it while her stomach spun with anticipation. Nobody was around. Most of the rooms on the very top floor were rarely visited and only used for storage. She picked the smallest one, slipped through the heavy door and wondered if it'd be stupid to open the roof window. Of course, it would be.

Boxes of old books and toys were stacked against one wall but the room was otherwise empty. She opened a box and waved away the cloud of dust which sifted up. Books. Her old books. Dreams and fiction. She was half-considering taking them downstairs and reading them again when she heard a sound outside and froze. If it was anybody but him -

"Fucking hell," Zed ran a hand through his hair as he entered the room. "It's hot up here."

He kicked the door shut, turned to slide the bolt across and then took a step closer to her. His eyes flicked to her mouth and then to her eyes.

"There's nobody around?" he asked.

Violet opened her mouth to reply but his lips caught hers before she could. He kissed her like it was all he'd ever wanted to do. His hands grasped her waist, pulling her closer as his mouth opened against hers. He held the moment for a second, as though waiting for her to make the first move and just as she moved her tongue, he moved his, swooping it into her mouth.

He tasted like mint and the urgent push of his tongue made her feel dizzy. It was so hot; she could feel the sweat on the back of her neck and her dress stuck to her back a little as he pushed her against the wall. He pulled away, his lips still hovering against hers.

"How long have we got?" His mouth brushed hers as he spoke.

She opened her eyes.

"As long as we need," she whispered.

Zed let out a breath, trapping her lower lip between his. "You don't even know how long I've wanted this," he murmured. "This. You. Being alone for real."

He kissed her again, his tongue more confident as it swept against hers and one of his hands traced upward into her hair, grasping a handful. His mouth moved down her neck, kissing the smooth skin, his tongue tracing the dip between her collarbones.

"You smell like heaven," he whispered.

His hand was on her face, almost rough as he traced the lines of her cheekbones and jaw. He straightened up, his fingertips pushing against her mouth and she parted her lips instinctively, eyes on his. He let out a harsh sigh as he slid his fingers deep into her mouth.

"You can't imagine the things I want to do to you," he said. Violet looked at him, pulled his fingers from his mouth and said, "Show me,"

He didn't hesitate. His hands went down, undid his belt and pants, and she reached forward instinctively, touching his hard cock. It felt hot even to her sweaty fingers and she wrapped her hand around it, stroking gently.

His tongue wet his lips. They were looking at each other, both breathing hard and the more her hand moved, the deeper he breathed.

"Get on your knees," he said finally.

She didn't hesitate. His hands sank into her hair as she took his cock in her mouth and he pushed forward. She looked up at him. His eyes were closed.

"Fuck," he sighed.

Her tongue curled against his hard, throbbing erection and

he slid further, guiding her head back and forth as he stroked gently in and out of her mouth. He went deeper with every couple of thrusts and soon enough, he was hitting the back of her throat. Violet sucked in air through her nose, her eyes watering as he moved faster, his breath coming out harshly.

"Look at me," he hissed.

Her eyes flicked up to meet his and he exhaled.

"Jesus fucking *Christ*,"

He pushed forward urgently, his cock going as deep as it could and he held her there for a few seconds before pulling back. She used her tongue on the underside, hoping to abate him but he pushed again and even though it hurt to take it, she didn't want him to stop. There was something reckless and lewd about the moment; something intensely satisfying in being used for his pleasure. She looked up at him through her damp eyelashes. His mouth was open, panting almost as he drove in and out of her mouth and when his eyes locked with hers, he let out a groan.

She wondered if he was going to come but before she found out, he was pulling free of her lips. He crouched down to her level, wiped the wetness from her chin with his hand and kissed her breathless mouth. His hands caught the hem of her dress, tugging it upward so he could feel the warm skin beneath and he detached from her mouth long enough to sweep the thin cotton up and over her head.

Nobody disturbed them. The room was furiously hot and the bare floorboards uncomfortable against their bodies but it didn't even occur to either of them. Zed's hand pushed between her legs, coaxing her to orgasm before she even had time to protest.

Then he pulled back, easing out of his shirt and pants. Violet took the opportunity to free her legs from the damp underwear tangled around her knees and had only just tossed the scrap of lace aside before he was kissing her again. His body was damp with sweat and warm above hers. Sweaty skin. She tasted the salt on his collarbone as he moved between her legs, fumbling through his discarded clothes for a condom.

"I should've brought my camera," he said, his eyes drinking in her naked body. "You're like a work of fucking art, princess." He kissed her again before she could laugh. Something about the way he touched her made her feel so wonderfully wanted. His hands groped her body like he wanted to remember every angle and curve and each time she gasped, he touched her harder, his fingers clawing and stroking against her until she could only moan.

By the time the head of his cock pushed against her, she didn't think she'd ever wanted anything more. He eased inside her slowly. Every movement felt significant. He filled her completely, to the border of pain but it could have been ten times worse before she protested. Her fingers clawed at his back and she felt fleetingly grateful for having short nails.

She'd wanted him. Wanted this. Dreamed of things she could never admit to but here, in the daylight, skin against skin, everything was beautiful and crystal-clear.

He pulled back and pushed again and she exhaled.

"Yeah?" He pushed her hair back and studied her

expression. "You like that?"

"I love it."

His hand went to her throat and curled around it, holding her in place as his hips lifted. She followed them with her own, half-afraid he'd detach completely but he pushed back hard enough, burying himself deep inside her. He ground against her as long as he could and then he pulled back again, his movements becoming a steady rhythm. With each thrust, Violet felt the hard floor against her ass.

There was nothing to do but take it. Take it and welcome it and revel in it. She didn't want it to end. Some part of her wanted to be there forever, running the fuck on repeat for eternity. His cock felt so right in her, natural and pure. Sweat. They were fighting for breath in the small, overheated room but they kissed again wantonly, mouths wet and hungry as his pulsing cock plundered into her over and over.

"You – feel – incredible," he growled, as he withdrew before slamming her hard against the floorboards.

"God!" The word spilled from her mouth. "Someone might hear."

Zed didn't stop. Each thrust was measured, forceful and her snatch only seemed to get wetter each time her ass hit the floor.

"Hear us?" He raised an eyebrow. "What? Hear me fucking you?"

She moaned as he pushed in deep and ground there, making pleasure flood her body. His hand groped a path down

her body and his fingertip found her clit, rubbing it urgently.
She sucked in a desperate breath.

"Zed – Please."

"Please what?" His hair was damp with perspiration and he'd never looked more attractive.

"Please fuck you until you can't walk? Please what, princess?"

"God," She couldn't hold his gaze as his finger moved. Her body felt as though it belonged to him; everything he did reverberated through her. She tried to suck in air but he was kissing her again, his tongue roughly exploring her mouth as his finger quickened. She couldn't hold on. Her body arched under his as she came, clenching hard around his cock.

"Fuck!"

Zed came too, his mouth dragging to her shoulder and biting down as he jerked inside her. The mutuality only intensified the pleasure. They ground against each other as his weight gave and for a long while, all Violet could feel was hot, draining satisfaction.

***

The days passed in a blur; endless boredom replaced by rampant fascination. Violet was so used to everyone knowing everything about her that when Zed returned her questions, she wasn't quite sure what words to give him. But it wasn't an interview. It was just them. Two people leaning into adulthood and getting high off the thrill of deceit.

Nobody knew. She couldn't begin to imagine what her father would think if he found out. It didn't bear thinking about. He had plans. Vague ideas coming out of an ever-present blurry mist about suitable matches his advisors been considering since her childhood. Violet knew the shortlist and it bored her to no end. The right men. The kind of men who spoke right and looked right and wore their clothes right and were so righteous it sickened her.

They couldn't compare to someone like Zed. There was too much going on. Too many falsities and good impressions and perfect accents. All the polishing had removed any character they'd ever had. Next to Zed, they were like washed-out watercolours beside a Leonid Afremov masterpiece.

She couldn't stop. Excuses piled on top of one another into a solid, impenetrable dam. Nobody suspected. Nobody would. After all, there was no reason why Zed shouldn't be around and they picked their places well, zigzagging between empty cellar and attic rooms and always timing their exits and entrances to perfection.

He took photos of her. He owned a camera which had cost more than his car and she teased him over how possessive he was of it.

"It's the most expensive thing I ever bought," he frowned.

"It's an investment, y'know? And it does so much, I fucking love it. Before I met you, I'd look at it and jerk off."

"Oh my god," Violet was in hysterics. "You must be joking."

"I'm dead serious," he smirked. "I don't even let anyone touch it."

Photographs. It made her uncomfortable at first but there was nothing indecent about the portraits Zed took. He wanted a face to practice on and after all he'd given her, how could she refuse?

Besides, it was as close as she could get to seeing herself through his eyes though something about it scared her. In his photos, she looked far more poised and attractive than she'd ever felt.

"This doesn't even look like me,"

"Who else does it look like?" he frowned. "Though the way we *think* we look is different to the way other people see us. Like in a mirror? That's a reversed image. And yeah, photos are still two-dimensional but they're more accurate, y'know?"

"You don't understand," Violet said. "I've had pictures taken of me since I was born. But yours are just – different."

He lowered the camera and frowned at her.

"Are you saying I'm not a good photographer?"

"No! I think you're great, honestly. I just – you're different."

He smiled the way he always did when he tried not to.

"I'm kidding," he said. "I don't even do portraits. More street stuff, really. I had some pieces in a coffee shop but nobody really gave a crap. Anyway, my old art teacher fixed me up with this gallery in Shoreditch. It's crazy popular. The show opens next Friday," He glanced at her, suddenly struck by an idea. "Hey, why don't you come?"

Violet frowned. "You know that's impossible."

Zed set down the camera and smiled.

"Nothing's impossible, princess."

* * *

Somehow in the darkness of night, it was easier for him to be honest. Vulnerability didn't seem to matter in the dark.

"Do you think of me?" Zed's voice was a creak, so quiet and yet so loaded. "Like, a lot? All I ever seem to do is think of you. Do you get like that?"

"Sometimes," she lied. The word came out soft and pointless. Did she think of him? All she ever did was think of him. It hurt. It ached. The nights alone made her cry. Long, late nights. Sleepless. Damp sheets and tears leaking into an already damp pillow. She found herself grateful that tears didn't stain. Too many questions.

"Are you well, Violet?"

They never used to ask. They never cared until Darren left. She still thought of him too, of the sudden end. How had they done it? Money? Or something worse? She fervently hoped they'd paid him off, given him enough cash to leave. The alternative didn't bear thinking about. Money. He'd always wanted to buy a motorbike. She liked to think of him in a foreign country somewhere, Italy perhaps, racing down clay streets on something noisy and obscenely pollutive.

   Maybe he'd met someone else. An Italian woman with long, dark hair and perfect tanned skin and a name like – like – Maria perhaps, and maybe this beautiful Maria sat on the back of the bike with her slender arms around Darren's waist as they went to a fruit market in Tuscany to buy tomatoes to make homemade spaghetti Bolognese.

   "Actually, spaghetti Bolognese is a British thing," Zed said knowingly. "Italians would be repulsed by it."

   They were lying in her bed, his fingers tracing the lines of her collarbone.

   "Excuse me for the culinary mistakes in my fantasy," Vi said.

   Zed blew out a breath.

   "Why'd you do this anyway? He'll never have met anyone who could compare to you."

   "I just – I just have to," she said and she didn't elaborate because he wouldn't understand.

   It had to be real. It had to be. Darren had to be somewhere in the sun, alive and planning out his whole future with Maria in a cluttered apartment which smelt like smoke and perfume and incense. Because maybe it wasn't true but there was a tiny chance that it was and that was what Violet's life had become; clinging onto the edges of chances, selling herself outrageous lies just to stop her mind falling to pieces.

Each lie was intricate and full of the essential details nobody would ever ask but her. And just beyond was the truth, a horrific thing, dark and encompassing, a hell-like pit and she couldn't even go near it, let alone do something about it. Somehow the mystery of Darren hurt even more than that of her own mother, simply because there was no end to him.

She'd touched him, felt his beating heart against her palm while her mother was just a shadow, a newspaper tragedy she couldn't even remember.

"So, this Darren?" Zed's voice. It was the most warming sound she'd ever heard. "He was the only guy you've been with?"

"Mm-hm."

"Do you still think of him?" His voice didn't catch on the question. Was he jealous? Vi doubted it. Something about Zed was far too full of life to get hung up on insecurities.

"Sometimes," she said.

The helpless truth lurked in the back of her mind. Darren wasn't the kind of guy who'd get paid off. He just wasn't. She closed her eyes. Or maybe he was. Maybe she'd been wrong about him. She'd been what – eighteen? Practically a child. Naive and gullible. Darren had taken the damn money and ridden off into his sunset with Maria. Darren. Her mind took off before she could pull back the reins and then she was gone, hurtling through the memories of him, the memories of them, the stolen nights, the stolen days, wind in her hair and his voice in her ear.

He wasn't perfect. Neither of them were. Too young. Too restless and greedy. And when it all came to an end, when he vanished without warning, the world seemed to lose colour. All the time after came in grayscale memories. His car. He drove a tornado red Seat Ibiza, an ancient nineties piece of engineering and when he'd left, his car hadn't. It'd stayed in the grounds for almost a week until it disappeared overnight. Details. They didn't add up to a reasonable number. Something about the little catches, the invasive uncertainties filled her with fear.

Zed shifted beside her.

"So Friday? It's on, right?"

Violet blinked. She looked at the ceiling, at the way the moonlight from the leaded windows fell across it in a warped chequerboard glow.

"I don't know, Zed. I really – it's so risky."

He didn't speak for a few seconds but she sensed his silent frustration and something about it made her feel guilty. She frowned at the ceiling rose, at the ornate chandelier suspended from its centre. The risk. The risk that he'd disappear into nothingness, just like Darren had. But she'd been furiously careful this time. They'd never even ventured out of the grounds together. Nobody knew. They couldn't know. And one night was feasible. The thought made her insides twist with anxiety but she swallowed hard. Wasn't he worth it? Wasn't he worth so much? Hadn't he brought life back into her existence?

"But what's life without risks?" she said lightly. "No risk, no reward, right?"

There was a pause.

"You're serious?" Zed's voice was already alight, and as he spoke it burned brighter like a flame tearing along a line of fuel. "Because I cleared it with my sister. Adrianna – she's cool, totally cool with it and she won't tell a soul. And nobody will know. Nobody will even think twice. And you know, even if they do, they're not the kinda people to make trouble, you know? We only want fun. We don't play those kind of games. You know what I mean? Games like – just those sick kinda games."

"Rich people games?" Vi offered, "Manipulation? Blackmail?"

"Exactly," he enthused and then added a belated, "No offence."

Was she offended? Could a reasonable person be offended by the truth? Was she reasonable? What the hell did any of the words even mean anymore?

***

Just another Friday night. Ralph would drive Violet to the orchestra, dropping off Zed on the way. The show would last a couple of hours. And then they'd drive her home. Nothing to see here. Move along.

Don't see the part where the car pauses too long outside Zed's apartment block. Don't see Violet go inside. Don't see her switch outfits with Zed's sister. Don't see Adrianna replace her in the back of the car.

It happened too fast. Clothes, sunglasses, hurried instructions and then Adrianna was walking out and ducking into the car. Violet tried to stay calm. Everything was under control. Nobody would pay Adrianna any attention. Why should they? She'd get to the hall, sit in the assigned seat, and listen to the music. They'd reunite after the concert, change clothes and then Ralph would drive Violet home. Besides, from a distance, her and Zed's sister looked similar enough. Long, dark hair and a similar height. If everything went right, the plan was perfection.

Perfection. Like Zed's hand, holding hers. There was an aching beauty in the gesture. She did her makeup in his car on the way to the gallery, going heavy on the eyes in a way she never did in public. Extra jewellery. Darker lipstick. Detractions.

"Relax, please," Zed parked on a street two blocks from the gallery and looked at her. "People see what they expect to see. We got this, Vi."

He was right. Nobody looked at her twice. She wandered around the gallery, high on the lack of attention. Nobody cared. Nobody watched her. They were far more interested in the art, the artists and Zed whose popularity caught him off-guard though his photos more than warranted it. They were breath-taking black and white snapshots of the city, so well-timed that people crowded around to look.

A pedestrian racing across a road in front of a furiously gesticulating lorry driver. A taxi driver looking back anxiously at a speed camera. A woman in high heels chasing a dog who'd broken free of his leash.

Everyone loved them. Everyone wanted to know him, to talk to him, to ask him about his influences, his experiences, the places he went, the camera he used, the college he hadn't attended. The night passed too fast, a haze of black dresses and champagne. Violet blended in and made small talk and by the time it was over, she wanted to do it again.

But there was no time.

It had been raining outside the glass doors and even though it'd stopped, a crack of lightning followed swiftly by thunder promised more.

"Shall we make a run for it?" Zed asked, glancing upward.

"Why not?"

But they were barely halfway down the street when the heavens opened.

He pulled her into the entryway of an abandoned shop and they stood there, breathlessly watching the rain. A man rushed by, clutching a broken umbrella. Across the road, the windows of a pub gleamed with light. A man stood under the awning, hurriedly smoking a cigarette.

Violet shifted her weight from foot to foot, anxious for the storm to pass.

"We've got time," Zed reassured, checking his watch. "Did you enjoy it?"

She looked at him and smiled.

"You were incredible," she said. "And don't just laugh. You were. You are. They loved you. Everybody loves you."
He kissed her right there in the doorway of the desolate building, the rain pouring down behind them.

"It's all you," he said. His voice had dipped into something lower and his hand tangled in her damp hair as he kissed her harder.

"You don't even know all the things you do to me," he murmured.

His hand slid under her dress and pushed between her legs before she could think of stopping him.

"You just make everything go – gold, Vi."

She tried to tug his hand away but he didn't move, his fingers strong and insistent.

"Zed?" Her voice was breathless. "Really?"

He kissed her again, his fingers slipping past her underwear and stroking her until she moaned into his mouth.

"This is crazy," she whispered.

"Is it?" He looked at her, his hair damp and his eyes alive. "Does it really matter?"

His leg was between hers, holding them apart as his fingertip pushed inside her. She couldn't even look at him. His finger slid further and curled. He eased it out, then pushed in two at once, making her gasp. His face was a shadow, his free hand still tangled in her hair. She leaned into it as his fingers slicked urgently, his thumb pressing against her clit.

"You like that?" His voice was a growl. "Does it feel good, princess?"

"Don't call me that,"

He kissed her again and her teeth sank into his lip until she tasted blood. He didn't try to pull away. His fingers didn't stop moving, the endless stroke and push making her stomach clench.

"You gonna come?" he whispered into her mouth. "Are you gonna come all over my fucking hand?"

"Zed, please," She fought for breath. "This is – I can't - "

"Give it to me," His voice was as urgent as his fingers.

"Fucking give it to me, Vi!"

As though she could help it. As though she could stop it. His thumb moved in a languorous circle, his fingers soaked in her warmth. She pressed her face into his neck, inhaled the sweat, the rain, the fading kick of his aftershave. In that moment, he was everything. Everything. His body pressed against hers, tight enough so she could feel the hard heat in his jeans.

"God!"

Everything felt hot and wet, clean and dirty all at once. Nothing mattered. The rest of the world was washed out with the rain, all she knew was Zed and his voice, the push of his hand, the heat of his body and the need in every breath. She clenched hard around his fingers, the orgasm building in waves of drowning pleasure.

"Zed. *Zed!*"

The urgent pleasure spilled through her. It felt like all she'd ever wanted. His fingers didn't stop moving until she came again and even then, she had to push his hand away to make him stop. He let go of her and they stood there, breathing hard. His hand was wet and he raised it to his mouth, cleaning his fingers.

***

They were late. The changeover was a haphazard rush and by the time Ralph started the car, they were almost half an hour behind schedule.

"This is too fucking close," he muttered.
Violet looked out of the window at the world racing by. Ralph drove fast, trying to make up the lost time and she hated herself for doing it to him.

"Too – fucking – close," he said again. "Do you fucking hear me?"

She opened her mouth but didn't trust herself not to start crying. There was something empty about being alone after the crowds, after the warm light, after Zed.

"I'm not doing this again," Ralph said. The car swung down a side road and he accelerated, tyres screeching in protest.

"This was the stupidest thing. I can't believe I let you talk me into it at all."

Violet still didn't speak. Streetlights sent flashing strobes of light into the car, illuminating the reflection of Ralph's face in the rear-view mirror. He caught her eye and she looked away hurriedly, not wanting him to see the tears.

"I'm serious," he said, and his voice was marginally softer.

"There's no happy ending here, Vi. Please wake the fuck up."

***

Wake the fuck up.

She woke the next morning, got washed and dressed, went to eat breakfast. Everything seemed fine. No questions. She almost believed they'd gotten away with it. Then her father arrived.

They ate together a handful of times a year and never at breakfast. But he didn't eat. He dropped down into a chair on the opposite side of the table. One of his ever-present companions obeyed some invisible signal and rushed to pour a cup of coffee.

"So," the King said. "How was the opera?"
Violet looked at him. He looked at her.

"It was – wasn't opera. It was an orchestra."

"Right," He took a gulp from his cup. "And how was it?"

"It was fine. Just – fine." Details. She needed details like she had in all the lies she saved up for herself but now, at the one moment it mattered, her mind had gone blank. All she could think of was Zed. His hand. The things he did to her. She looked blankly down at her toast, her mind racing.

"Uh – it was a young conductor, actually," Her voice wavered a little and she fought to normalise it. "A prodigy. About thirty years old, I think. He was educated at the Royal Academy, actually. I think he got a scholarship."

The King seemed unimpressed.

"And how long did this show last? From what I've heard you were back late last night."

He could see the lies. She knew he could. But did he know the truth? She looked at him. Did he even care about her beyond what she represented? He sighed and looked away. She tried to eat but felt she might be physically sick. She reached instead for her own coffee.

"Sometimes, Violet, you remind me far too much of your mother,"

One sentence. He didn't even look at her as he said it and half a minute later he'd left the table and disappeared with his mob of advisors. Violet's hand was shaking so much, she dropped her cup. It smashed on the cold tile floor.

***

She had to end it. There was no other solution. She couldn't deal with another disappearance. Her thoughts went to Darren. He'd paled into insignificance since Zed had arrived but the pain still lingered. She couldn't let it happen to Zed. There were too many people. She thought of the newspaper stories she'd read about a mother she hadn't even known. Boating accident. Too young. A convenient death for an inconvenient woman.

In the attic room, Zed tried to get her to smile, his precious camera endlessly snapping pictures.

"Come on, princess. You know I've sold hundred of prints since last night?"

She looked at him. His easy smile. His untidy hair and his perfect face.

"Congratulations," she said. "You deserve it."

"You could sound a little more psyched," he frowned, adjusting the camera. "Gimme one smile. One. That's all I want."

He crouched down beside her, the camera too close to her face. She pushed him away.

"Stop, Zed. Just put it away. Please."

He sighed but switched the camera off.

"Fine. D'you mind if I leave this here just for a few days?" He held up the camera. "Ade's boyfriend's moving in with us and he's an ex-addict. I don't trust the bastard."

"Fine. No one comes up here anyway."

"You're sure?"

Violet sighed. "Yes. Honestly, you love that thing too much. I'd buy you a new one if you lost it anyway."

Zed narrowed his eyes.

"It took me five years to save up for, Vi. I earned it. It kinda means a lot." He laughed self-consciously. "Sentimental bullshit, I know, but I guess -"

"I get it," she cut him off.

He frowned and she turned away, looking at the old books neatly boxed away. Her head hurt.

"Vi? Are you okay?"

Ralph's words from the night before were all she could think of. *No happy ending.* He was right, of course. Everything they were doing had a time limit. Soon enough it'd have to stop. The pain would hit sooner or later. There was no way to avoid it.

Zed had put the camera away. His hand touched the back of her neck and she pulled away.

"No. We can't do this anymore, Zed. I can't."

Her throat hurt with every word. She picked up a pristine paperback and flicked through it.

"Is this 'cause of yesterday?" Zed asked. "I mean – sure we almost fucked it up but it all turned out okay, didn't it? It's not like anyone found out. And it was a one-off. Why would it even change anything?"

Violet didn't answer. She looked down at a random page of the book. The words were blurry.

"Hey," Zed's hand came out again, touching her bare elbow this time. She pulled away and he exhaled. "For fuck's sake, Vi. Why are you doing this? What have I done wrong? I'm not asking you for anything more."

She swallowed hard. It hurt too much. Everything always hurt. Her eyes were already wet and she blinked away the tears, wondering what she'd even do with her days now. Life before Zed seemed like a distant memory, a listless, lonely place she didn't ever want to see again.

"Vi, come on."

He looked at her pretending to read the book and let out a controlled sigh. He reached out, snatched the book from her hands and threw it onto the floor.

"Fucking talk to me. What is it?"

Violet paced to pick up the book and then left it.

"My dad was – I don't know," The words spilled out desperately. "He's acting differently. He knows something. I can't do this. It's like the past repeating itself."

"How would he know?" Zed frowned. "He can't know."

"Well, he knows *something*!" Violet's voice broke and she turned away. "We can't. I can't. I'm sorry."

She unlocked the door and ran down the stairs before he could stop her.

***

He didn't stay away. Late night. She knew he'd show up like he did on any night he could and even though she dreaded it, relief flooded her at the sound of his voice.

"You're overreacting," His voice on the other side of her bedroom door. She didn't open it but found herself standing beside it, desperate for contact. "Your dad doesn't know. We don't have to end this."

"Stop it," Her voice was thin and useless. "You know how stupid this is."

"Do you think I give a fuck?"

"I'm not doing this again," She tried to sound assertive. "I'm not. It's selfish and sick and I can't, Zed. I'm going to bed now."

"No you're not," he said. "And it's not selfish."

"Do you even – do you have any idea what we're doing? How stupid this is?"

"What's he gonna fucking do, Vi? We're not doing anything wrong!"

"You're even more stupid than I thought," she said and waited for him to be offended. He wasn't.

"Let's just get out of here," he said. His voice came through the door and eased into her. She pressed her forehead against the cool wood.

"What do you mean?"

"We'll just run away," he said, like it was that easy. "Just fucking get out of this hell. We could go anywhere. I don't know. Where d'you wanna go? France? Italy? Morocco? I'll take you there. I'll take you anywhere you fucking want, princess."

"Shut up," The idea was so beautifully ludicrous she couldn't bear it. "Shut up, Zed."

He didn't speak for a while, though she knew he hadn't left. She felt his presence and when he finally did speak, his voice was low.
"Let me in, Vi. C'mon. What's the harm?"

"I like you too much," It was the truth and it hurt her physically to say it. "I like you far too much and this is all going to blow up in our faces. I can't have it. I can't have you. We should stay away from each other."

"But why?" His fingers were tapping out a soft, inconsistent beat on the door. "I don't mind keeping it quiet. Why can't we just be together? Just us? No one has to know. Ever. No one will ever know."

Violet swallowed hard.

"You think? You really think they won't know? How many people are in this already, Zed?"

He paused like it was a trick question.

"Just- us, right?"

"No. Me. You. Your sister. Ralph. That's four, Zed. And we can't do this without Ralph. What happens if he leaves? If he accidentally tells someone else? We've already taken too many risks. My dad knows. I swear he already knows!"

"Hey," Again, the seep of his voice. It was like cool water under the endless glaring spotlight. "Hey. He doesn't know a damn thing. Ralph's cool. Ade's cool. We got this."

But they didn't have it. They didn't have anything but a fragile web of intricate deceit and sooner or later it'd be torn apart. If she'd learnt anything about her own life, it was that nothing stayed secret for very long.

"God, Vi. You're killing me. D'you know that? It makes me hurt so bad."

His words were her emotions and she couldn't bear it.

"Stop, please."

He didn't.

"I just – I want you forever. Is that such a bad thing? Nothing means anything without you. I sold so many goddamn prints and it's empty, Vi. It's nothing if I can't share it with you."

"You don't need me,"

"How the fuck would you know?"

She closed her eyes tight, trying to stop the tears. Everything was pain. Anxious, terrifying pain. Was anything worth anything? Did it make sense to push away someone she'd already allowed to come so close?

"Let me in," he said. "What's the difference in being on this side of the door?"

They both knew the difference but she couldn't say no. She opened the door. He stood leaning against the wall outside. They eyed each other warily.

"Don't slam it in my face," he said. "People might hear."

"You're not funny," she said.

He straightened up and stepped into the room, shutting the door behind him.

"If I could stay away, I would," he said. "I swear I would. But I can't, Vi. And I'm not gonna apologise because what the fuck. What the *fuck*. We both want the same thing."

He kissed her before she could speak and they stumbled across the room onto the bed. Every kiss was desperate. All they had were secrets. A relationship balanced on an unstable stack of worn lies. There was no sense in plans, in ideas or fantasies. There was just now. Now. This moment. The dark bedroom and his hands pulling off her t-shirt, dragging her shorts down her legs. His shirt on the floor and his jeans next to it. A wrangle of sprawling bodies. His cock pushed insistently inside her before she could even tell him how much he meant to her and even then he didn't let her speak, his mouth covering hers every time she opened it. Her legs went around him, making him go deeper, making her eyes water at the intensity of each urgent thrust.

"How can you want to stop this?" His eyes were accusatory.

"Do you even know how much it hurts?"

If he'd have let her speak, she'd have told him she felt the same but even as his mouth left hers, his fingers replaced it, sliding deep until she moaned around them.

His pulsing cock felt like heaven, driving away all the doubts and fears. With each packing thrust she fell further into the moment. He pulled his fingers from her mouth to grasp at one of her tits and she took the opportunity before he stole it back.

"It hurts me more than you know," she whispered. "I can't even tell you, Zed. I just – you mean the world to me."

"I do?" His finger and thumb found her nipple and tugged at it. "Really, princess?"

"You know you do."

His cock was stationary inside her and he pushed harder, trying to get deeper still. His free hand slid beneath her, under her ass and she squirmed as his fingers moved, skimming across her asshole.

"Zed – what're you –"

He pulled free of her snatch.

"I wanna fuck your ass,"

Violet swallowed hard. He'd said it before, countless times but it'd always been easy to laugh her way out of it. Tonight, everything felt heavier, darker, more insistent.

"Zed, please."

"C'mon, princess," he whispered. "Don't you wanna give me everything?"

They kissed, mouths open, tongues swirling in a tangle of wet desire. He was everywhere, occupying all her senses. He knew how to touch her; knew the way to get between her legs; where to bite, where to stroke. Sometimes she felt like nothing more than an instrument beneath him.

He sat up above her, leaned to the bedside table and extracted the ever-present tub of Vaseline. She didn't stop him. She didn't want to, didn't dare to, didn't want to do anything but make him happy. He slathered the lube onto his hard cock. They watched each other silently.

"I don't care who your fucking father is," he said, eventually. "I don't care what he thinks. This is us. Why should anyone get between it?"

"I know," Her voice was like an inconsequential shadow. "And I wish it wasn't like this."

He eased his weight off her.

"Turn around."

She obeyed wordlessly, her heart pounding. His hand went between her legs and curled around her snatch, his fingers dragging wetly over her star. He pushed her legs wider apart. All Violet could feel was the thump of her heart. Her fists clenched as the head of his cock pushed against her asshole.

"Relax," His hand pressed hard on her lower back. "Just let it go."

She swallowed hard, her fingernails digging into her palms. He pushed harder, pulled back and pushed again. She heard the box of lube thump softly onto the carpet. Zed's hands went to her hips as he pushed. It didn't take as long as she expected. Once the head of his cock had entered, her passage seemed to relent and the rest of his pulsing dick slid in easily enough. It felt like nothing else. There wasn't a pain she could pinpoint, but a long feeling of stretching violation.

"Is that okay?"

"I – think so."

He pulled back and she gasped into the sheets, her hands clutching at them desperately.

"Zed – I - "

He worked with short strokes until the alien feeling subsided. His hand moved around to press against her dripping snatch as he increased the pace. She could hear the heavy grate of his breathing and he leaned over her as he moved, his mouth pressing into her neck.

"You feel like heaven," he growled.

Violet couldn't speak. She turned her head to the side, sucking in lungfuls of air. Her fingers sweated as they clutched at the bedsheets and the harder he went, the faster her heart beat. It felt too good. Too dirty. Too nasty and yet so beautiful. It wasn't anything she'd ever fantasised about or contemplated but with Zed, it felt wonderful. He moved faster, his body smacking against hers.

His fingers were working against her, making her body reach for release and when it finally came, she felt as though she might expire from the force of it. Everything was a blinding, scorching mess and she tried to close her legs, tried to feel it for what it was but Zed was still there. He was still thrusting even as she clenched and she could feel his breath against her neck as he rasped out dirty, intelligible words. His hand didn't stop moving until she came again, her snatch soaking his fingers.

"Zed, please!"

She didn't think she could take any more and thankfully, he couldn't either.

"Fuck!"
The word came out of him with a jerk as he forced himself deep inside her, thrusting desperately as his cock finally gave in, spurting urgently into her depths.

"Fuck," he hissed the word again, his face pressed into her neck as he dragged in air. "Fucking hell, Vi."

They were both shaking.

***

The following morning, Violet looked out of the second-floor window from where she could usually see him patrolling the gate. He wasn't there but there was someone new, someone more heavyset with blonde hair. She frowned, scanning the guards scattered along the gates outside. Nothing.

He'd left before she'd woken, leaving no trace of his ever being there, bar the languorous aching of her body. But he always left early; his regular shift started at seven and he had to find a way to make his way out without arousing suspicion. She pressed her forehead against the glass, scanning the sporadic row of guards again. Maybe she'd missed him – maybe -

"He's gone, Violet,"
Ralph's voice. She turned.

"What?"

"Zed. He's gone," Ralph stepped closer. "Apparently he handed in his notice. He got a gig at some magazine."
Violet turned back to the window. The glass felt hot against her forehead. She stared down at the gardeners slaving in the September sunshine.

"What magazine?"

The pause hung between them, soft and fragile.

"I – I don't know, specifically." Ralph said, "I figured – well, I thought you'd know already,"

She turned without a word, walked quickly past him and back down the corridor to the one guest room which looked out onto the staff car park.

Zed's car was gone. Something like relief filtered through her but it wasn't enough. It trickled hesitantly, far too meagre and insufficient to wash away her doubts. He wouldn't. Things like this didn't make sense. Did she want to know? Did she dare to find out, to ask questions, to feel a greater pain than abandonment could ever cause?

It'd be easier to accept Ralph's words. To be heartbroken and betrayed. And yet she was turning from the window already, her mind too full of thoughts to work coherently. She rushed out of the room, down the carpeted corridor and ran up the main staircase, past empty rooms and empty people, past all of it to the stairs up to the attic and she was too far gone to care who might see.

Her shoes were loud on the solid stone steps. Higher and higher. Hotter and dryer. Dustier and dustier. All of it seemed stupid now; immature dreams and fucks, the pathetic life of a bored princess. She stopped at the very top of the stairs, steadying herself on the bannister. Something about the heat made her feel weak in a way she'd never felt before.

She didn't want to know. She didn't want to look. But she was walking down to the very last room, their room, the place they'd come to call their own. She pushed open the door. The book he'd thrown the day before lay abandoned on the floor. She didn't touch it. She walked numbly to the corner and leaned over to lift the lid of the box where he'd stored his precious camera, hoping it'd be gone. He wouldn't leave without it.

Please be gone.

It wasn't gone. It lay in the box, sleek and gleaming, unaffected and proud in its inanimateness. Violet replaced the lid. She blew out a long breath. The feeling inside her was cold. She felt detached, like what was happening couldn't really be happening, like she might just wake up from a bad dream. But it wasn't a dream. Moments like this were never dreams. Her nightmares had never surpassed the revulsion of real life.

It'd take her a while to come up with a sufficient explanation but she'd find one. She always did. It had already started. Money. Of course. Money made the world spin. They'd probably given him enough money to buy a hundred godforsaken cameras. She pressed her thumb and forefinger to her eyes and tried to stop the flow of tears.

The End of Nothing

The woman sat on a foldable chair on the corner of Drew's street, a stack of magazines in her lap and a cardboard sign propped up beside her.

> **The Weekly**
> **2.50**

A laminated card pinned to her clothes read:

> ***Arta Orsos***
> ***Licensed***
> ***Vendor***

Ms Orsos was old and draped in a mass of shawls and blankets. She looked up warily as Kaia halted in front of her and then looked away, apparently satisfied that there was no way she'd be able to extract a sale. Kaia frowned. She'd been down the street countless times but had never noticed the magazine seller before. In fact, she probably still wouldn't have if it hadn't been for the picture of Drew and Alana on the top magazine cover. She looked in her bag for change and found nothing smaller than a ten.

"Hi," she said, and held out the money.

The woman eyed her hesitantly before taking the cash. She seemed confused for a second but came to soon enough and went to extract a magazine from the plastic packet in her lap. There was something remarkably gentle and graceful about the way she slid the magazine free and yet Kaia somehow knew it wasn't something she did very often. Or at least, often enough.

"Thank you," Kaia said and took the magazine. She looked down at the cover, then folded it in half and stowed it into her bag. Arta Orsos didn't look for change and Kaia didn't ask for it. She stood there awkwardly a moment as both of them avoided looking at each other and then she turned hastily, heading for Drew's building. Once safely past the doorman and inside the elevator, she retrieved the magazine. *Childhood sweetheartsTo power couple.*

The front page picture was airbrushed perfection; Drew helping Alana out of a sleek, black car. She wore a deep blue, knee-length dress, her blonde hair lifted by the wind, her smile as flawless as the rest of her. Kaia stared. She looked closer at the magazine, wondering numbly how one woman could be quite so beautiful. It almost made her panic. She opened the magazine. *Andrew Sanderson: The Person Behind The Politician*. More pictures. Too many pictures. Laughing faces and diamond jewellery, champagne and suits and his hand on Alana's waist and then on her neck and then in her hair.

The elevator stopped and the doors slid open. Kaia walked the few metres to Drew's apartment and pushed hard on the buzzer. The door opened almost instantaneously and he stood in front of her, his belt undone and his shirt nowhere in sight.

"I thought you weren't gonna show."

He looked at the magazine in her hand.

"Where the fuck did you get that?"

"A woman on the street."

He took it from her, tossed it onto the floor and then kissed her hard enough to take her breath away.

"It's been too long."

He always had the same line but it always felt appropriate. He pulled her through the door, closed it firmly behind her and then pushed her up against it so he could kiss her. Her mouth opened instinctively and his tongue pushed in, searching urgently.

Nothing ever felt like it was enough.

His hand went between her legs and pressed hard enough to make her moan. Kaia's eyes closed. She pushed back at him, the pressure almost too beautiful. His fingers moved beneath her underwear until skin met wet heat. She bit her lip hard and he let out a long breath.

"You wanna come? So soon? I've hardly even touched you yet,"

"I know, I know," Her words rushed out breathlessly. "But it's been too long."

His fingertip had pushed inside her, his thumb pressing hard against her throbbing clit. The sweat felt like it was evaporating from her heated skin.

"I fucking love you," he murmured. "Every millimetre of you. I just want to be inside you all the time."

"You talk too much," Kaia whispered but she didn't mean it because every word from him hit her like a sugar rush, sweet and addictive. He knew how to talk. He knew the words, the things to say, the way to make her insides clench and her snatch drip around his searching fingers.

She couldn't look at him. His forehead was pressed to hers and if she'd opened her eyes, she knew his would be there; the ocean blue dimmed to a rainstorm as he watched what he was doing to her. It was almost unbearable. Too much. She knew what she'd see and yet seeing it in her mind was almost as bad. The clench of his jaw, the way his dark brows would be pulled together. She saw his face in every fantasy she ever had. The same expression. Heat and urgency.

"Look at me," he murmured, like it was simple.

She didn't. His fingers slid inside her, curling into the tight heat of her entrance until the heel of his hand pressed against her. He pulled her towards him with his fingers inside her like it was a decent thing to do. Kaia gasped. Her snatch leaked copiously around his hand.

"I feel so numb without you," he said. "But when I push my fingers inside you, it's like I'm alive. Like life is in colour again."

"Save your bullshit for the voters," Kaia whispered and she felt his whole body smile.

His fingers were moving inside her, coaxing her towards a release and though it took everything she had, she reached down and pushed his hand away so she could drop to her knees before him. When she looked up at him, his fingers were already in his mouth. Her hands moved hastily to undo his pants. The hardness beneath them seemed glaringly obvious, dangerous almost in its demand for attention.

"I really thought you weren't coming," he murmured.

"Why wouldn't I?" Kaia looked up at him, her hand wrapped around his throbbing cock. There was something beautiful about feeling him shudder under her touch.

"I dunno," His voice was a rasp. "Just - life, y'know?"

"Life." Kaia repeated the word softly, her hand stroking the length of his hard cock. She looked up at him, extended her tongue very deliberately and circled the pointed tip around the head of his cock.

"Does Alana go down on you?"

Drew exhaled carefully. His hands were clenched into fists.

"Like hell she does,"

Kaia closed her lips around his cock, her eyes never leaving his. It was just a moment but it hung between them, so familiar and yet not familiar enough.

"You are so fucking beautiful," Drew hissed. Kaia almost rolled her eyes and then realised the effect might be lost with his cock in her mouth. His hand gripped her hair hard as he pushed further along her swirling tongue. His hand tightened the more she took but there was a perfect pressure in the pain; the press of his fingertips and the pull of her hair felt somehow cathartic. She wanted to ask him to pull harder even as her eyes watered.

"All I do is wait," he said. "It's like I'm just doing things to fill all the empty time, going further and further for the tiniest buzz. I just wait. For this. For you. It's the only thing that makes me feel alive."

He pulled her up so he could kiss her again. His hands fisted in the skirt of her dress, pulling it up. They broke apart long enough for him to drag it off her and then they were kissing again. His leg was between hers and she could feel his cock trapped between their bodies, hard and insistent against her stomach. She wanted to touch it again, hold it in her hand and feel the way he throbbed for her but he caught her wrists before she could, holding her arms back so her body arched harder into his.

He bent, kissed down her neck, along the flow of her collarbones until he was too low and dragging her down to the carpet with him. He let go of her hands to fumble through his pockets for a condom and she untangled her damp panties from around her legs before moving on top of him.

He looked at her like she was delicate. Feminine and soft and beautiful, like a summer cloud or some form of spunsugar. His hands fumbled between their bodies as she leaned down to kiss him and then he was pushing, pressing his cock against her until the moment hit and her body lowered against his. His cock stretched her so completely that she couldn't tell who was throbbing harder. Kaia pressed her palms flat against the carpet either side of him and pulled back until he was barely inside her before moving down until he was buried. He pushed back, making her take it deeper until their bodies ground desperately against each other.

"Jesus," His hands went for her, pulling her down urgently so he could kiss her, his fingers sinking into one of her breasts as though kneading the weight of it could vent his frustration.

"This is everything," he hissed. His hands slid over her body, digging into anything he could hold onto as she rode his cock and moaned into his mouth.

"Harder," his voice groaned. "Just – do it harder."

She did. She met his thrusting hips for every packing stroke. His hands dug into her ass and he moved suddenly, rolling her onto her back so he was on top. Their eyes met. He kissed her with his hand around her neck until she thought she might never breathe again. But she did. The air felt crisp and quenching as he pushed inside her until her eyes watered. He fucked her hard, driving each thrust into her like he was trying to knock the air out of her lungs. She was breathing so hard, her head spun. Her nails dug into his back, her ankles crossed at his tailbone. There was nothing like being under him.

Her body took all he could give until she came, writhing beneath him on the carpet. His cock stilled momentarily inside her and when she opened her eyes, he was looking at her, his jaw clenched.

"I fucking love watching you come," he rasped and his hand went between her legs as he thrust hard again, bottoming out inside her. The weight of his body trapped his hand against her clit and he rubbed it as he ground his cock inside her. She came again, her lithe body gripped by pleasure and Drew came too, his body like an earthquake around her as he jerked repeatedly. For a while, everything was pleasure until it ebbed away and all she wanted to do was hold onto his warm body until she fell asleep. But she couldn't. He moved off her reluctantly and they lay there, breathing hard.

She never knew what to say when it was over. Two people and reality and a whiter than white ceiling. Outside the windows, rain had accelerated the sunset. Streetlights glowed in the drizzle. She felt Drew look at her.

"What's wrong?" he asked.

Everything, she wanted to say.

But why ruin the silver sliver of time with him? Why fill the seconds with fighting?

Instead, she smiled.

"D'you remember when we were like seven, and we took your bed sheets into the garden to make a fort?"

Drew laughed. "God, how could I forget? My dad was fucking livid."

Remember when? Remember when? It was all she did anymore. Hanging onto lifeless memories, even as they faded like old newspaper. Remember when. And she couldn't remember anything new anymore. She'd find herself repeating the same things she'd said last year and one year later didn't have nearly the same effect as twenty years later. It'd become stale; forced, desperate conversations to fill the aftermath. Sometimes she thought it'd be easier to walk out straight after.

Would it? Instead of staring at the ceiling and hating her own voice as she tried to make him laugh.

Remember. Why live in the past? Because the present was unbearable. She could hardly face herself in the mirror anymore. Things had gone too far, farther than either of them had ever planned.

She stood up and put on her dress.

"So – next week?" she asked.

Drew sighed.

"I wish. I'm not sure. Everything's about the election right now."

"I still can't believe you've become a politician."

He smiled as he stood up.

"What, don't I look the part?"
"No, you're perfect."

He laughed, stretching as he headed for the bathroom. "I wouldn't go that far."

She left while he was still in the shower, picking up the discarded magazine she'd arrived with and stowing it in her bag. She'd learnt long ago that attempts at goodbyes only felt self-servingly awkward.

Back on the street, it was dark and busy. The magazine seller had disappeared.

"Excuse me? Kaia Porter?"

She stopped en route to her car and turned to see a dark-haired man. He extended a hand. She didn't take it.

"Can I help you?"

"I'm Matt Gold, from The Era. I'm writing a feature on your friend, Andrew Sanderson and was hoping-"

"Andrew Sanderson isn't my friend," Kaia interrupted. She frowned. "How do you even know my name?"

"He's not your friend?" Matt's eyebrows went up a fraction. "What, so you work for him? 'cause you just came from his place, right? And you were both at Waterstone High? You grew up, what – four blocks apart?"

Kaia blinked. The man smiled innocuously.

"I don't know what you think you know about me," she said, haltingly. "But you're wrong. I don't want to talk to you."

He nodded like he'd been expecting it.

"That's absolutely fine," He dug through his pockets. "But wait – one sec – here's my card. You just call if there's anything. Anything."

Kaia looked down at the card, put it into her purse and walked quickly away.

***

She read the magazine she'd bought from cover to cover. She even did the puzzle page Sudoku and made an attempt at the crossword. Every so often, she found herself flicking back to the piece on Drew and Alana. She couldn't help it. She stared at the pictures until they blurred into pixels and then she blinked and stared at them all over again.

Alana Redgrave. His wife. His 'childhood sweetheart'. Kaia rolled her eyes at the headline. *Childhood.* Kaia was the one who'd known Drew since childhood. Alana had arrived ten years later and she was only ever meant to be a temporary part of his life. Something about getting her big shot father to drop a lawsuit against Drew's parents. Kaia could hardly remember the reason now, only the way life had played out since.

Alana was the kind of girl who spawned insecurities in every other teenage girl. Blonde and bronzed and beautiful. Chemically beautiful. She smelt like strawberry flavour. Not real strawberries but a confectioner's idea of strawberries, beautiful for the most part but with a manufactured over-sweetness. Kaia barely knew her beyond the crowded school corridors. She wasn't even vaguely interested, at least until Drew was.

"It doesn't mean anything," he'd said, "It's just something I have to do. It's not as though I actually like her."

They were skipping gym class, killing time behind the science block. They never had anything to do. No money. Nowhere to go. Just bodies and conversation.

"She likes you though, doesn't she?" Kaia said and it was true. Alana had always had a thing for Drew, inviting him to her birthday parties even though the rest of her friends were repulsed by his social circle.

"Look, I wouldn't go near her. You know that. You're the only girl I've ever wanted. It's just to help my parents. I mean, I go out with her, she gets her dad to drop the case, we're done. That's all, Kaia. You get it, don't you?"

"Of course I get it," Kaia said, and she did. "It's just – she *really* likes you."

"Not *really*," he'd said and the faint uncertainty of those two words was all it took.

The weeks played out. Kaia would see him and Alana together, holding hands, and talking with their heads tilted in private conversation. But afterwards he'd laugh, tell her about all the mind numbing things Alana and her friends talked about; movie stars and matte lipsticks and how many washes a temporary hair dye actually lasted. Alana was a means to an end but the end seemed to extend, going further and further into the distance until there was no closure in sight.

Maybe Kaia should have stopped it; extracted herself from the situation in the early days but it never seemed like Alana would last. Her and Drew were so fundamentally different. Alana's parents were rich, her father a lawyer who owned his own firm. Their family came from the side of town Drew vandalised. And yet, day by day, that side of him seemed to fade. Teenage dreams gave way to real plans; to college applications and internships at law firms. He had an image to keep up, people to impress, places to go. Kaia saw less of him but it only made time together more thrilling.

Months wore on. School became college; classes and days interspersed with stolen phone calls and painstakingly planned hours together. He always said the right things. Always put a time limit on whatever he had with Alana but as spring spilled into summer and the semester ended, he seemed further away than ever.

He played golf and tennis and spent long summer Saturdays at garden parties and even longer evenings at dinner masquerades. He wore suits and combed his hair and ate at the right places so as to get photographed at the right places. After university, it didn't stop. His graduate job was at Redgraves - working under Alana's father - and to anyone but Kaia, he looked like he fit right in.

Was he still there? Under the Savile Row suits and clean-shaven smile? Of course he was. He'd come over, drink milk straight from the bottle, straight from the refrigerator, and when he laughed it was the same laugh it had always been, the one that made Kaia feel as though living had a reason.

Around her he was the same. Endless phone calls. She couldn't remember how many nights she'd lain awake, phone clutched to her ear as they talked about anything and everything for hours on end. School and dreams and music and movies and books and parents and ways to meet up and steal time like they were doing something wrong. Was it wrong? He'd been hers far longer than Alana had been around. And yet, Kaia was the secret. Drew would pick her up at midnight, headlights off and radio turned down to a whisper. Sometimes they just drove. Aimlessly and endlessly. Smooth black tarmac. Inky blue sky. On a clear night, they'd walk on the beach, long after the surfers and joggers had gone home and the sand and water were open and serene and the world looked like it stretched on forever. The thought scared her as much as the mass of words tumbling out of Drew's mouth the fateful night after his engagement hit the local paper.

"It was just something I had to do. If I didn't, it'd have looked like I wasn't committed and you know I have too much riding on this. I need the money, Kaia. My dad's medical bills are through the roof."

"But you're not actually going to get married, are you?" Kaia felt colder than the October ocean. "Can't you just – find an excuse? We'll move away. We can go anywhere we want."

"And do what? I'm making good money here. I won't get another break."

"Money's not everything, Drew."

He ran his hands through his hair and exhaled.

"I know. I know, okay? But – it makes everything easier. If you don't have to think about it, you can live, y'know?"

"And this is living?" Kaia looked at the deserted beach. "This? Lying and hiding? This is what you want from life?"

Drew exhaled. His hand felt warm around hers.

"Of course not. It'll work out, okay? This isn't forever."

"But it *feels* like forever. I don't want this. I've spent the last five years waiting for you to end it and you're just taking things further. I mean, you must like her, obviously. Do you?" Her voice carried in the wind. "Do you love her?"

Drew scoffed. "Alana? Of course I don't fucking love her. She's like glass."

"But you tell her you love her?" Kaia persisted. "You lie to her, and you fuck her, and you live with her, and now you're gonna marry her. I can't deal with it, Drew. I can't do this anymore."

She'd meant it. She'd left him on the empty beach and walked the three miles home in the dead of night and when he called the next day, she didn't pick up. She deleted his voicemails without listening to them and then lay awake night after night, wondering what he'd said. Life became emptier than ever and a month later, the inevitable arrived in the form of a gold-embossed ivory envelope. She opened it, extracted the wedding invitation and stared at it until even the hollow shell of her life cracked and fell apart.

***

She made a decision not to go to the wedding, then changed her mind and bought a dress more expensive than her car. She took hours to perfect her hair and makeup. As though it mattered. As though she had something to prove. The wedding was an exquisite midsummer affair; the ceremony took place outdoors on the beach and the reception in an enormous marquee strung with hundreds of fairy lights and filled with hundreds of guests. Kaia knew maybe a dozen of them. The rest were from Drew's other life; people who called him *Andrew* and drank champagne like it was water.

It went on late into the night, dancing and drinking in a riot of champagne and confetti and wealth. She shouldn't have stayed so long. She should have made pleasantries and left before sunset. But she didn't. She made the wrong decisions that she always seemed to make around him and at a quarter to midnight, they were alone on the outside of the marquee, inches away from the music and laughter and it felt like they were in a different world altogether.

"You came," Drew said.

The way he said it opened the door for a joke, an icebreaker, but Kaia didn't take it.

"I guess I should congratulate you," she said.

Their eyes met and he held her gaze unashamedly.

"Look at you," she said softly. "All dressed up. You've been with these people so long you've just become one of them. And all this time I thought you still got it. But you don't. You don't care. You just got married. To Alana fucking Redgrave. I can't even – you're such a *liar*. You actually married her."

"Like it fucking matters," Drew said, "She's just a woman. Me and you are more, y'know?"

Kaia stared at him incredulously.

"You are so full of shit."

"I am? So what are you doing here? Did you dress up like this for anybody but me?"

His dark eyes went down her, hard and hungry.

"I could fucking eat you up."

"You can fuck off."

He caught her wrist before she could walk away. "Easy, princess."

White-hot anger flared behind her eyes.

"I'm not your fucking princess, okay?" She jerked free of his grasp. "It's pretty obvious, *Andrew*. You've got your fairytale. You act like your hands are tied but somehow it's all worked out. You've got your beautiful fucking wife and your money and your life and your penthouse castle, okay? Alana's your goddamn princess, not me."

If only she'd ended it there. If only she'd held tight to the rage, stalked away and left him alone. But the anger tripped, faltered, wavered on the cliff-edge and before she could help it, she was hurtling down into pain. Pure pain. The pain of ten years of secrets, of being nothing in the daylight.

"Baby," Drew's voice spilled into her. "Baby, I'm sorry."

"I don't care!" Her voice broke like a chain stretched to its last limit. "I don't fucking care."

But she cared. It was blindingly obvious. He pulled her to him and his arms went around her and he felt so warm and familiar that she couldn't even pretend to fight. His mouth crushed hers desperately, as though he needed her. Did he? Why would he fake it? She bit his lip until he bled and even then he didn't stop kissing her.

"I missed you," he hissed against her mouth. "You can say what you fucking want but I'm dead without you. And you're the same. We can't live without each other."

"You're so full of yourself," Kaia said, but saying it to him made her want to cry even more. "I don't need you."

"Yeah? You don't?" His hands had slipped beneath the skirt of her dress and dragged a path up to her ass. His fingers dug into it hard. "So where's your date? Why're you here alone, baby?"

He kissed her again and she kissed him back, half drunk and fully desperate.

"I hate you," She poured the words into his mouth but as clear as they were in her own head, all either of them heard was gasping.

There was nothing to lean against, nowhere to go. They fell onto the sand, almost fighting each other in their haste to feel skin. Her hands dragged his shirt from the waistband of his pants and pressed against the smooth muscle underneath. He always felt so warm. Inches away, the party went on; music loud and shadowy silhouettes moving and dancing. Laughter and alcohol.

Drew moved between her legs, dragging her dress up around her waist. He didn't kiss her again. He fumbled with his pants, freed his hard cock and pushed her underwear aside so he could push into her. He groaned even louder than she did, his face pressed into her neck.

"You feel like home," he said and his voice ached.

She wished it wasn't so easy. Sometimes she wished her body would take over and reject him but it never did. His cock made her fit around it and it felt like all she could ever want. He ground harder, his hand going down to grasp her leg and pulling it wider so he could get deeper and then he was stroking in and out of her until she didn't want it to end.

She didn't look at him and he didn't look at her. She clutched at his shoulders and tried to push her body back at his. But he was going too hard. Each thrust felt like it could push her through the sand. She reached for him instinctively, sank her fingers into his damp hair and kissed him like it could ever convey what he did to her. He groaned even as his tongue curled against the wet heat of hers. His cock moved harder and deeper. His teeth bit her lip as if to return her earlier favour. Kaia moaned.

"Aren't you gonna come, baby?" His voice was desperate enough to push her over the edge. She clenched around his thrusting cock, her eyes closing tight as her body shook with rippling spasms. Drew jerked moments later, his mouth still on hers and it felt as though he'd never been closer; almost as though he was pouring his soul into her body. For those few moments of frenzy, it felt like all was right with the world. But then she opened her eyes. The night sky was dark and starless. Sand was stuck to her arms and legs. Drew's weight was heavy above her, his breathing loud. Inside the marquee, the wedding party went on, clueless and jubilant.

Drew shifted. He moved back, rearranged his clothes, dusted himself off.

"I'm not doing this again," Kaia said.

Drew looked at her, sand in his hair and resignation in his eyes.

"Like either of us can help it."

***

It had been crazy at first. Day after day, lies, excuses, endless risks. And then gradually, it had quietened off. Every other day. Every week. Every other week. Still an addiction, but a sensible one, kept at bay, far out enough for nobody to notice.

But it was too far out now, in danger of drifting away altogether.

Drew hadn't texted for weeks. Kaia scrolled back through their conversations, played his voicemails on loop. She typed a text. Backspaced. Tried again. Threw her phone down and stared at the ceiling until her eyes watered. How much hurt would it take for her to stop? To walk away? Why couldn't she?

The buzzer sounded and she sat up. A delivery? A friend? Neither.

"Hi," Matt Gold said, when she opened the door. His eyes were gold, she thought distractedly. Like his name.

He smiled. "Can I come in?"

Her hand tightened around the door handle.

"You're harassing me."

He frowned.

"I'm sorry."

"No you're not."

"I am, actually," He looked down at the scratched laminate floor and then directly at her. "I'm very sorry for you, Kaia."

His presumptuous use of her name felt indecent.

"What's that supposed to mean?"

He shrugged, a frown creasing his face.

"What does he give you? It's not money. It's not love. What is it? Empty promises?"

Kaia swallowed hard.

"You don't know anything."

"Maybe I don't but sometimes it's good to get a fresh perspective, isn't it? And the way I see it isn't all that pretty."

"Nothing's pretty," The words came out unintentionally wistful.

Matt's eyes flickered over her. "He just doesn't like you very much. At least not as much as you like him."

His opinion hurt her more than she could stand. She tried to feign disinterest. She looked out of the window at grey snow drifting down. Her head hurt. Her eyes hurt. Everything inside felt out of place, uncomfortable and twisted.

"I'm sorry," Matt said. "But it's true. Why else would he do this? He doesn't care, Kaia."

She stared at him. He looked back undeterred. He was a stranger. A journalist. A stalker, practically. Why hadn't she shut the door in his face?

"You think you and him are ever gonna live happily ever after?" he asked. "That's a joke, Kaia."

"How would you know?" she said and immediately regretted it. The words were practically a confession.

But Matt merely shrugged.

"It's pretty obvious the way I see it. Sometimes if you step back, things are really different."
Kaia didn't look at him. She couldn't look at him for fear she might just fall apart.

"You just want an article," she eventually said and shut the door before he could protest.

Could she suffocate from loneliness? She leaned against the door and looked at her neat apartment. Pieces of her life. It looked so empty she could hardly breathe. One crazy part of her wished she'd invited Matt in and made coffee for him and talked to him about his life and his job and his name and anything and everything to kill the crippling silence of solitude.

She escaped from nothing and stood in line at the

supermarket checkout, lost in other people's conversations. The girl in front of her was texting; the guy behind her soothing his tantrum-throwing toddler. Everyone seemed mildly irritated at life, at the indecency of having to be alive. Campaign posters were plastered everywhere. She stopped at a lamppost and looked at the airbrushed picture of Drew. *Vote Sanderson.*

Back in her dented car, she looked blankly out of the windscreen at people heading to and from their vehicles; harassed-looking parents shepherding children, carts overflowing with toilet paper and fruit and cereal boxes and tabloid magazines. People reading stories of other people when their own lives were spilling over with meaning. So many lives. So many crushing stories.

She found herself driving down Drew's road, knowing it was crazy but unable to help herself. The traffic moved in a loose queue and on the sidewalk she noticed the woman she'd bought the magazine from almost a month ago.

Unthinkingly, she pulled to the side of the road and bought a magazine for no good reason. She only had a twenty and the vendor looked in her small cross body bag for change but Kaia stopped her.

"It's fine."

Arta Orsos looked faintly insulted.

"Not charity," she said. Her accent was Eastern European maybe and her voice soft.
"It's not," Kaia said. "I don't like carrying change."

She wasn't sure if Arta understood but she seemed satisfied enough to stop rifling through her tattered bag. A cat was with her today, sitting beneath the chair and eyeing Kaia with sea green eyes. Kaia wanted to touch it. She also wanted to go over to Drew's place, press his doorbell and see the look on his face when he saw her. She didn't do either. She crossed the road, got back into her car and drove home.

***

He texted eventually. Twenty nine days since they'd last met.

Tomorrow 4pm?

The words captioned a slightly blurry but very graphic picture.

He sickened her. But even more sickening was the rush of relief flooding her body. Beneath the hatred, beneath her furious glare at the screen was the rush of warmth she always got from his attention.

She raced through the next day, leaving work perilously early. She put on a new sleeveless dress, did her makeup like a Maybelline tutorial and layered up edges of perfume clouds. She felt giddy. Nervous. How could she get nervous about seeing a man she'd known for twenty years?

As ever, she parked her car a good few blocks from his place, and walked the distance. On the way, she suddenly remembered the magazine seller and rifled through her purse relieved to find a twenty. She found herself wondering what the woman did with the money. Food? Rent? Did she even have a home? Children, maybe? All of a sudden Kaia wished she could give her more but it was too late to find an ATM and besides, she doubted the woman would even accept anything over a twenty.

But in the end it didn't matter, because Arta Orsos wasn't there. No magazines. No chair. No trace. Kaia looked around, did a three-sixty right there on the sidewalk, scanning endless pedestrians for a face that matched. Nothing. The cat she'd seen last time appeared from beneath a parked car and mewled pitifully. The sound made her ache.

"Kaia?"

She turned to see Matt Gold smiling lopsidedly.

"You look nice," he said.

Kaia rolled her eyes.

"Looking for Arta?" he asked unexpectedly.

"You know her?" Kaia frowned.

"Of course. I've been parked out here tryna dig up dirt on Sanderson for weeks. She sold me magazines. Told me when the parking inspector was coming."

"So where is she?"

Matt shrugged.

"Maybe you should ask Andrew."

"What's that supposed to mean?" Kaia snapped.

Matt shrugged again. He crouched down to stroke the cat and it purred with delight. Kaia glared at how beautiful they looked, then turned and walked quickly towards Drew's building.

When he opened the door, he was drafting a speech. Sheets of paper were scattered around the living area.

"It's kinda the final rush," he explained. "Another week and that's it."

Kaia took off her coat and glanced down at his scrawled handwriting. It was as indecipherable as it had been at school.

"I saw the polls," she said. "You're way ahead."

He moved past her to shut the door.

"It's been too long since I saw you. You okay?" His voice dipped like he really cared. Did he care? Kaia watched him pull off his t-shirt and almost felt ashamed of herself but before the thought could settle, he kissed her. His teeth sank into her lip and tugged until she opened her eyes and looked into his. His hands were at her waist. The same hands that'd been touching her all her life and yet they suddenly seemed like something woefully precious. Something she wanted to hold onto and examine until she'd committed them to memory. She pressed her mouth harder against his so he released her lip and kissed her properly.

His fingers found the zip on the side of her dress and he tugged it down until the material hung loose and he could push it down to fall around her ankles. His thumbs hooked into her panties and eased them over her hips until they dropped free. He broke the kiss, his eyes darkening as they flickered down her naked body. He swallowed, his Adam's apple moving in his throat, just below where his dark stubble faded out. It looked like the most masculine thing in the world.

"Do that again," she whispered.

"What?"

"Swallow."
The needlepoint of a smile threatened but he obeyed and she felt like she could come just from watching him.

"Again," she whispered.

"Fucking hell, Kaia."

He spun her around and slapped her ass, startling her. She almost gasped but caught it in time. His fingers sank into her cheek, kneading the firm flesh before he spanked her again. Kaia swallowed hard. Her snatch felt like it might start dripping. She arched her back, presenting her ass to him.

"Harder," she whispered.

He hesitated.
"Harder?"

"I just want to feel you forever."

His fingers went between her legs, massaging her snatch until her body clenched in anticipation. Then he spanked her again. Hard. Her skin heated and he did it again and again until her eyes watered and she flinched in expectation.

"Fuck, Drew!"

"What? You asked for it."

She heard him fumble with his pants and looked over her shoulder at him. Their eyes met. It felt like they were full of secrets, like they knew one another like nobody else ever could.

His body pressed against hers and she turned her face back to the wall. She felt him shift so his cock pushed between her legs. She pushed back at it desperately and they ground wetly against each other until the frustration was dizzying.

"Fuck," Drew pulled back, his breathing was rushed.

"Condom."

The clinical, careful moment. A drop of sanity in an ocean of madness. He grasped her wrist, pulling her through into the bedroom. The bed was unmade. She sat on it cautiously, watching him rifle through the dressing table. He didn't take long and then he was on her again, creasing the sheets as he pushed her up the bed and caught her legs so he could push inside her. He didn't go slow but slammed himself inside her, making her body adjust to take each throbbing inch.

"You're so fucking tight," he hissed. "It kills me."

Each thrust was hard and packing and made her insides clench. Every time she thought she might come, he slammed

in deep again, the impact bringing reality back. Nobody made her feel as good as he did. He drove deep and ground against her, making her arch in pleasure. His mouth covered hers, stealing every moan and gasp as his hips shunted back and forth. His hand went between her legs, slipping over her snatch as their bodies moved. He pressed his fingertip against her clit, rubbing it until she clenched desperately around him. She was soaked in sweat. Her pulse raced; she could feel it everywhere as her body writhed beneath his, the endless throb and twist of pleasure coursing through her.
"God, Drew."

His hand still worked against her, his cock moving all the faster and more erratically as he chased his release. By the time he came, Kaia was clenching around him all over again, the release radiating from her core. She was aware of the convulsive jolts of his body as he emptied himself, his face pressed hard into her neck. They didn't stop moving against each other until they had nothing more to give. And then it was over. Drew pulled back, moving to lie next to her.

The sheets smelt faintly like strawberry flavour. Kaia tried not to think about it.

"Fuck." Drew's horrified voice cut into her thoughts. "Fuck, Kaia. I think the condom broke,"

Her mind raced for a terrifying couple of seconds. Calendars and days and weeks and -

"I – I think we should be good."

"Shit! You sure?" His voice poured with relief.

"Yeah. I think so. Yeah."

"Thank fuck."

They lay in silence for a few seconds. On the bedside table was a neat stack of campaign flyers. Kaia picked one up, her heart still pounding. *Vote Sanderson. For our children. Our hospitals. Our schools.*

"If it was though," Kaia began hesitantly. "What would we even do?"

Drew sat up. "But it's not. It doesn't matter."

Kaia swallowed hard, still looking at the flyer.

"But if it was," she pressed. "Hypothetically. If we were unlucky."

Drew looked at her.

"We couldn't."

The silence stretched between them, cold and uncomfortable.

"So – when you come on the TV and say all this stuff about being pro-life?"

"Pro-life in a reasonable way," he corrected, like he was fielding questions from a press room.

"And this would be *unreasonable*?"

Drew ran a hand through his hair. He looked at her hard.

"You wouldn't actually *keep* it?"

Kaia looked back.

"Why wouldn't I?"

He held her gaze as though to figure out if she was joking and then he laughed.

She didn't join in.

"How did you become – THIS?" she asked.

"I haven't become anything, okay?" The laughter disappeared. "Can you stop? You don't know, Kaia. You don't understand!" He took a second to compose himself and then he looked at her. "It's just tactical, okay?"

He always caught himself before he snapped. She wondered if he was extra careful around her, if he only tolerated her because of the things she knew and the power they gave her. The thought made her sick. It instantly had the scope to turn everything they had from love to mere sex. Like a twenty year old hooking up with a rich old man. Fake affection.

"You've changed," she said, finally. "Sometimes you play a part so long that it becomes reality."

"What are you saying?"

"I don't understand why you're doing this," She looked at

him. "I mean, you've always had excuses, reasons, things to justify whatever you've done. Alana and her dad and everything. But this? The election? It's unnecessary. What are you getting from it?"

She got up and went to find her clothes. She started dressing hastily, suddenly unable to bear being naked around him.

Drew followed her uneasily.

"Why're you wrecking this? I thought you loved me."

"I thought I knew you."

She looked in her bag for a hairbrush and came across the money she'd intended for Arta. She looked at Drew. He looked at her.

"Let's not fight," he appeased. "I feel like-"
"There used to be a woman outside," Kaia interrupted. "On the street, selling magazines. Where's she gone?"

Drew frowned.

"Why'd you ask?"

Kaia shrugged.

"Just wondering."

He exhaled.

"We had the television cameras coming and sure, I'm all for

taking in refugees but can you imagine the field day the right would've had with an immigrant beggar on my goddamn doorstep?" He blew out a breath. "Jesus."

"So?" Kaia felt cold. "Where is she?"

"I don't know. Immigration came. She was illegal. Probably at a detention centre. I don't really care."

"You don't *care*?" Kaia knew her voice was wavering but she forced it on. "Your *parents* were illegal, Drew. Don't you remember where you came from?"

"I don't care. I don't live in the past, okay?"

Kaia opened her mouth and closed it again. There'd never been anything but sex. And she almost couldn't bear to face everything that'd been swept under the rug. How could she begin to reason with someone so unreasonable? Did she even know him?

She walked to the bathroom, locked the door behind her and washed her hands three times over. Her eyes flickered to her reflection in the sparkling mirror. Mascara tears. She didn't try to stop them. She gripped the edge of the sink hard and looked blurrily down as inky tears dripped onto the white porcelain.

Did she love him? She didn't want to believe what he'd become. But how long had it been? How many excuses had she made? She swallowed his lies like a child ate candy and now everybody else believed he was some saviour, some wonderful rags-to-riches luminary. But he wasn't. He was a liar.

She could hear him rehearsing his speech.

People ask why I'm doing this. And I'm doing it for us. For our city. For us.

Us. Our children. Our hospitals. Our schools. The selfishness dizzied her. Us. The truth lurked behind the words. Everyone else was a leech, a problem, an extortionist, trash to be disposed of. Like Arta. Harmless and homeless.

Could she stop him? Should she?

She had the means. She had everything. The evidence was overwhelming; endless text messages, voicemails, pictures, videos even. But could she? Could she betray him so brutally? It seemed incredibly cruel, an enormously disloyal thing to even consider. And yet if she didn't, she knew life would go on the same; praying for his phone calls even as he strayed further from the boy she'd known. It wasn't something she could turn off. It had to be destroyed entirely.

She left the apartment without saying goodbye. On the street, she rifled through her bag for Matt Gold's card and dialled his number before she could have second thoughts. He picked up on the first ring.

Lost Angels

Some memories don't stick. They're not important or consequential enough to make a lasting impression. But I remember Aiden. Everything about Aiden. For the first time in my life, in my messed-up shunted around excuse of a life, I felt as though I'd found someone who came from the same place.

We were young. Young and angry and selfish and dangerous. I think we felt as though the world owed us something. It was easy to make that assumption, especially when we were wandering around Los Angeles, wide-eyed and hungry.

We were always hungry back then. I'm not sure what for. Success. Excitement, maybe. We'd slope down the streets of Bel Air, Brentwood and Beverly Hills, shirts and hair damp with sweat as we looked at everything we didn't have.

There's no harm in looking. We saw the wealth, the homes, the cars; everything jutting out, offensively on display like a porn-star with over-enhanced tits. There was something both sickening and extraordinary about it.

Summer had set in. The rich families had gone on vacation. The houses lay empty. Big, gated residences with pretty gardens. Palm trees. Balconies and pools. We'd see the maids go in, the pool cleaners, and once a week, the gardeners. They worked in a perfect routine.

We timed it. Picked the easiest house. Waited until the maid left. Ran around the back, pushed through the tall hedge and cut a hole in the wire fence. It tore a scratch in my leg, made the blood trickle down to my ankle.

Pristine white sun loungers were out by the pool. It was secluded, private. Aiden caught the hem of his t-shirt and pulled it off. He kicked his boots off, unzipped his jeans, stripped down out of his boxers and dived in one perfect arch into the pool.

"Fuck!" he gasped, surfacing. "Get *in* here, Lise!"

I didn't need to be told twice. We swam up and down, raced each other, luxuriating in the clean, perfect water.

"Imagine if we actually lived here," I breathed. "If we were like this rich couple with all this to ourselves."

"But this isn't us."

I looked over my shoulder at him. "What, you mean we wouldn't flaunt our wealth?"
He scoffed. "*No*, I mean, I'd have a round swimming pool, not a rectangular one."

I smiled, warming to the fantasy.

"We'd eat breakfast. Like croissants. And champagne. And strawberries."

"Caviar?" Aiden suggested.

"Uh-huh."

"I'd drive a Ferrari." He jumped out of the water and sat on the edge of the pool, naked and dripping wet. "A blood red

Ferrari. I'd drive it to work. Some useless job somewhere. The kind of office with free food. On the weekend, I'd play golf."
I looked up at him, my chin balanced above the surface of the water.

"I'd play tennis."

His smile lifted. "In all-white? Like the short skirt?"

"Exactly. At some exclusive club."

He smirked and splashed water at me.

"Would you make sex noises every time you hit the ball?"

"Maybe," I splashed him back. "If I played with you."

"And at night we'd fuck in like a bed of money. Just money," Aiden's eyes closed, his face tilted up to the sun. Everywhere. Flying all over the place. Drifting down. So much fucking money, Lise."

"And everyone would know us and want to be us."

"And we'd laugh behind their backs."

"Cause their houses would be smaller than ours."

We laughed as though the whole idea was too ridiculous, as though we would never want to do that kind of thing and yet underneath, we ached because we always wanted everything.

People who have nothing want everything. They want money and parties and country club passes and fancy dinners and expensive clothes and more than anything, they want other people to give a damn about them.

We fucked right there by the pool, my mouth finding his cock first. It never took long to turn him on. In fact, I privately believed he was always half-ready, sex just beneath the surface, ready and waiting patiently like an appliance on standby. His fingers wrapped into my damp hair as I sucked on him and like he always did, he waited a little while before taking over to guide my movements.

"You're fucking incredible," he hissed.

I *felt* incredible. I felt beautiful. I felt as though I could do anything, be anyone, but all I wanted to be in that moment was myself, doing exactly what I was doing. He pulled me up, dragged my mouth to his and kissed it hard.

The sun filtered through the palm trees and soaked into me, into Aiden's broad back. I felt his shoulder blades, the way they jutted out, still waiting for the bulk of maturity to settle into. The edge of adulthood. He knew me. He'd been my first and I was certain he'd be my last as well as everything else in between.

He fucked like it nourished him; urgently and desperately, his hard cock driving into me over and over. His hands touched me in a way no-one could ever hope to match, grasping my tits, my neck, fingers gliding into my mouth as he watched, slack-jawed. His lean, warm body pressed against mine, his mouth hungry as ever, his fingers skilled and knowing. Sometimes I thought I could come from just having him look at me.

We lay there a while after we were done, gasping and sweaty until we found the energy to get back in the pool. When the shadows became longer, the sun receding, we dressed, wandered away from the pool to luxuriate in the huge park-like garden.

The grass had been cut and watered and we could smell it, that perfect, perfect scent. The gardener had left everything immaculate but to our amazement, he'd also left the basement door unlocked. We went inside like we owned the place. The basement was almost empty, lawnmower and garden tools to one side, bicycles and boxes of crap stacked against another wall. It would be too good, wouldn't it, for the door into the house to be open? Surely, we couldn't be that lucky? But we were. It was open.

We fell into this palace, this gold and cream furnished heaven, flat screen TV's and wall lamps and soft fucking furnishings. We wandered around in a wealth-induced haze . The place smelt like money. It literally smelt like banknotes. The kitchen looked like it was from the future, marble, glass, stainless steel and polished granite. There were eight bedrooms, six bathrooms.

Chandeliers. Cinema room. Glass walls. Home gym. Signed sports memorabilia. A wall full of wine bottles. Movie props. A fucking *bowling alley.*

We didn't trash the place, partly because it seemed a waste, but mainly because we didn't want to get the maid in trouble. We ate small, sensible amounts of food from the kitchen. If we'd have known how to open champagne bottles, we'd have drunk some. We washed in a palatial bathroom and came up smelling of sweet lemons. In the master bedroom, I found a walk-in closet bursting with clothes, fancy names on the labels that I couldn't even pronounce.

I put on a Caroline Herrera dress, and raided the rooms until I found a matching pair of heels in my size. I found MAC and Elizabeth Arden cosmetics and made-up my face ecstatically until I looked like I could possibly belong in Bel Air. I found Aiden wearing a tuxedo and trying on cufflinks.

"How'd I look?" I asked, leaning against a glossy white doorframe.

He glanced at me, eyes a little guarded like he didn't quite recognise me.

"You look – like a magazine version of yourself."

I pouted. "Is that bad?"

"No," he shrugged, still frowning. "But I like you the regular way."

The view from the huge window looked out onto the sky-scraping city, buildings and palm trees, a sweeping vista of wealth and fantasy.

"I almost feel like we belong here," The words tumbled out of my mouth before I'd decided to say them.

Aiden glanced across at me, his eyes dancing. "Wanna test that theory out?"

We hit the White Temple, a pretentiously overpriced fusion cuisine restaurant in Brentwood. The waiter gave us a quick onceover before his face melted into one big smile. He started working his tip the moment he opened his mouth. I could only imagine the way he'd have acted if we'd come in our regular clothes.

We ate charred rib eye and shrimp fried rice. Coconut ice cream. We'd eaten the exact same meal in Chinatown a few months back and the bill had been a modest forty bucks. At White Temple it came to two hundred and thirty. Needless to say we got the hell out of there as soon as we'd finished eating but not before Aiden had swiped a valet ticket from the neighbouring table.

"You get the car," he said, handing it to me. "I'll be out when you're ready."

I stood outside the restaurant nervously, waiting for the valet to bring out the car. A black BMW. It gleamed like treacle. I glanced into the restaurant; saw Aiden still lounging at our table making small talk with the waiter. I got into the car, kicked off my heels and put it into first. Half a minute later, Aiden yanked open the door and fell in.

"Go!"

I went. I didn't even look in the rear-view mirror. Aiden twisted in his seat, laughing wildly at whatever scene was going on behind us. We drove all night, hitting Sunset Boulevard for the fun of it, driving along the whole road and back again, debating how long we had before the car started showing up as stolen. We joined the Pacific Coast Highway in the early hours, flying over mile after mile of smooth road.

"Faster!" Aiden yelled. "Burn this motherfucker up!"

The car's purr became a growl. *Bring it on*, it seemed to be insisting, *bring it the fuck on. You think I can't handle you? Bring it fucking **on**.*

I drove so fast that the road blurred and every part of me was sick with anxiety. I clutched the steering wheel with sweaty fingers, the exhilaration making me breathless. I eased off the gas as slowly as I could, and yet it still seemed to take forever for the world to come back. They say the greatest moment of danger comes directly after victory and maybe that was what happened. Maybe I was relieved enough to get complacent.

As I slowed, the car skidded, control spiralling away as it lurched into the next lane, as out of its mind as Aiden and I. It happened so fast that it only comes back in flashes of panic. The BMW smashed against the highway safety barrier and bounced off. For a minute we were frozen, too shocked to move. Bizarrely, the car ended up facing the right way, having done a complete 360. It'd felt like a 720. I wondered if we'd died.

Aiden heard the sirens first and he looked over at me, rolling out the muscles in his neck.
"Lise? You okay?"

The cop cars came closer, lights flashing, red, blue, red, blue. We sat there in our stolen clothes in a stolen car, high on stolen food and a smile passed between us. We staggered out of the car like a pair of drunks and ran as fast as our shaking legs would allow.

It was a week before we found the nerve to pick up another car. We sagely agreed that Aiden would be the designated driver.

* * *

"Let's go somewhere else. I'm sick of the sun, Lise."

We were wandering aimlessly around the STAPLES store on Sunset, killing time and soaking up the free AC.

"Where?" I asked.

"I don't know," He rattled a box of paperclips and set it down again. "Anywhere. Let's just get the fuck outta here. I think we've taken as much as we can."

We didn't have much in the way of possessions. A bag of clothes between us. There really was nothing stopping us, nothing to stick around for.

"Okay," I said. "Let's go."

Aiden went out to find a car to start us on the road. I used the last of the small change we'd found in the BMW to buy food. Water. Potato chips. Peaches. I waited outside. I had become rather attached to my stolen high heels and wore them even with my white t-shirt. The traffic was loud and busy, the heat inescapable. I paced up and down, trying to be inconspicuous. Where the hell had Aiden gotten to?

I finally saw him coming towards me. In a goddamn Lamborghini. God knows where he'd got it but he could hardly drive it. It sputtered down the road like it was out of gas and people were looking, *staring* in fact, and I covered my face with my hands, unable to believe his how blinded he was by greed. What the fuck was wrong with a nondescript Ford? We only needed to get the hell out of town. We weren't going to the fucking Oscars.

But at the same time, I couldn't blame him. There was something so sleek and beautiful about that car, something that looked like money and comfort and carelessness. I could hardly wait for him to pick me up, could hardly wait to sit beside him in that ridiculous machine, to have him put his foot down until life and death were just words and all we knew was speed. Faultless engineering and sheer speed.

I waited impatiently, jiggling my weight from one foot to the other. I started towards him, too piqued to wait and such was my haste that the heel on my right shoe snapped, making me stumble and twist my ankle. I swore, snatched the left shoe and broke that heel too so they were even but by then it was too late. I was far too late.

I straightened up but a black and white LAPD patrol car had pulled up in front of the Lamborghini. God. I watched breathlessly, the sun beating sweat down on me. Aiden. For fuck's sake. I willed him to run. But it was a goddamn Lamborghini. He couldn't even get the door open. By the time he'd stepped out of the damn thing, another patrol car had pulled up. Four cops. I saw Aiden's eyes dart to me, saw him scan for an escape even as he reached into the car to procure registration papers.

The cops watched him lazily, smugly, arms folded across their chests, chewing gum and smirking at one another. I moved towards the scene numbly. Aiden shot me a look of warning. I felt the cops look at me in my shirt and broken heels, groceries clutched pathetically to my chest.

"Is there a problem, miss?"

They waited for me to say something. One of them muttered something. Three of them laughed loudly.

Aiden started forward, already losing it. He had a dirty mouth when provoked. The three officers stopped laughing and looked expectantly at the fourth who seemed to be their superior. Aiden was still running his stupid, beautiful mouth. He insulted them, their mothers, their daughters, as well as their family pets. They didn't seem amused anymore.

The fourth cop reached for his handcuffs.

***

A kilo of cocaine, they claimed. In the pocket of a jacket Aiden hadn't even been wearing. Something about the outrageous lie made my heart thump and echo like it was empty. Helplessness. I'd always thought there were some things that just couldn't run. Lies. Lies. And there we were, caught in a system that hated the fuck out of us and for what? For the cars? The food? For playing house? Or just for our sheer arrogance?

One kilo meant more than simple possession. It meant intent to supply which meant jail time.

I knew Aiden. I knew the dust he came out of. I knew he'd learnt to walk in a place where the adults were too stoned to walk. He didn't touch drugs. Not even goddamn weed. Not when he was raised in the low, clammy aftermath of a high.

I phoned seven criminal defence attorneys. They said one kilo in small bags was most certainly intent to supply. They didn't believe it had been planted and even if they did, there was no evidence. They said the same senseless things. Were Aiden's rights violated during the arrest? Was it entrapment? Did he even have any character witnesses? They weren't interested. There wasn't enough money to ever interest them.

***

He got off lightly, they said. No previous convictions. Eight years. It may as well have been eighty.

. I visited him the Saturday after he got sent down. He wore an orange jumpsuit and handcuffs which were roughly removed once he sat down. His eyes were tired. One of them had become swollen with a purple bruise.

"It had to happen sooner or later," he said. His smile fell to one side like it always did. He reached out as though to take my hand but his knuckles bumped against the glass screen separating us.

"You should – uh – do something," he said vaguely.

"Something real, y'know? Like get some decent work and have a place to sleep and all that." He dropped his voice. "I holed up some cash. Buried it in the place we met. For a rainy day, y'know?"

I looked at him blankly. "It never rains here."

"It will," he said. "So you go get it and I don't know. Play 'em at their own game, huh? You can do that, can't you?"

"I don't know," My voice sounded lost. "I don't know anything."

"You can. Shut up, Lise. You know you fucking can. You know the place. Listen to me, damn it!"

I couldn't look at him. I felt suddenly drained of life. For the first time in so many aching years, I wanted to cry.

"It's at the edge. You get in on Seventh Street at the corner. The gate. Five forward. Seven down. Inclusive. It's on the left. You hear me?"

My eyes flicked up to meet his and something in his jaw tightened.

"Don't you cry. Fuck everything else. Just don't, Lise. Don't cry. Please."

I blinked, tried to reply. There were no words that didn't come with tears.

I felt a hand on my shoulder.

"Excuse me, miss."

I turned. The cop's face was lined, old, and grey like his hair. Just a guy doing a job.

"Lise Cooper?" I nodded wordlessly. "Lieutenant Johnson wants to speak with you back at the station. I can drive you down."

I saw the frown on my face mirrored on Aiden's. He shrugged, tried for a smile. I stood up, followed the cop out of the room and didn't look back.

*　*　*

Lieutenant Bill Johnson was the same man who'd put the cuffs on Aiden. He smoked cigars. A heavy wooden box sat on the table in front of him; big, fat cigars with little gold bands around them. I watched him puff on one. He watched me watch him and shoved the box towards me.

"Help yourself,"

I didn't take one. The office was large with a big window. A fan whirred silently on the ceiling. I looked at the plaque on the big, mahogany desk. William S. Johnson. Gold letters. He was maybe twice my age. The face of a self-righteous bastard. Uniformed. A small silver bar had been pinned to each collar of his dark blue shirt. He saw me notice the pins.

"I'm a lieutenant," he said. He chewed gum even as he smoked the cigar. "Homicide."

I frowned.

"You were there when Aiden was arrested."

He inclined his head in silent agreement.

My frown didn't fade. "Why'd you wanna see me?"

He blew out a cloud of whirling smoke and eyed me. "You know, a lotta people go missing in LA. Lost angels, y'know?"

I didn't say anything. I waited.

"And I get these calls, all desperate for me to close a case," He flicked ash off his cigar. It landed next to my broken shoe. "Now, a couple weeks ago a body was found on the beach. Early morning. Guy had been robbed and shot. I ain't got a clue who done it. But y'know, sometimes there's this pressure to just solve the damn case. Could've been anyone. Could've been me. Could've been you. Or could've been some young guy off his head on drugs."

His eyes met mine. They were so blue, I felt as though I could see through them.

"I can make it happen. Nobody worth anything gives a damn about a small-time criminal. Maybe his DNA was found on the victim's shirt. We're talking – what – twenty five years minimum? Say he's provoked into bad behaviour on the inside. Life, maybe?" He leaned forward, his forearms resting on the table. They were covered in dark, coarse-looking hair. The hair on Aiden's arms had always been soft, sun-bleached.

"*Life*, Lise," Bill Johnson said my name purposefully as though to reiterate the fact he knew it. "You ever saved a life before?"

The room seemed very small. All I could smell was cigar smoke. It seeped into me, suffocating and blinding. I blinked, tried to look at him through the fog.

"What do you want?"

I knew the answer before he'd said it and even then it surprised me. What would a guy like him want with ME? I thought of Aiden. I thought of myself. Childhood. Dark rooms and blinding sun. Always on the run. We didn't give up. We could've given up years go. We didn't. We endured. We survived. We played them at their own fucking game.

Bill told me his address, said I should get my things together. It didn't seem helpful to tell him I didn't have any things. I stepped outside, ready for the heat to hit me. It didn't. The rain hit me instead, drops falling warm and hard. I thought of Aiden's cash. I thought of the hair on Bill Johnson's arms.

Life. What more do we have than our lives? I'd always worn selfishness as a mark of honour but as I made my way down the puddled street, it seemed to wash off, taking with it my identity.

* * *

I named the canary Blue. It sat sullenly on the perch in its large-but-not-large-enough cage in Bill's living room. It would always try to bite his fingers. I fell in love with it and it with me. A week after I'd moved in, it ate out of my hand.

"Don't ever let it outta the cage," Bill instructed. "Or it won't come back. It's waiting, the little son of a bitch."

I let it out of the cage every time he went to work. It flew joyously around the room and through into the kitchen, the bedroom, the bathroom. At six, a half hour before Bill came home, it'd fly back into the cage and cock it's head expectantly, waiting for me to lock it in. It could've flown out the window, could've had its eternal freedom but it didn't. I liked to think we were in cahoots. But perhaps it just stuck around for the free birdseed.

I cleaned the cage every day, lined it with newspaper, washed it with soap and water and refilled Blue's food and water supplies. I cleaned everything. The place was a mess the first day. By the end of the week it gleamed. I knew how to keep house. I'd spent the first sixteen years of my life running around after an alcoholic grief-stricken father. But I never resented him. I loved my father. It hurts when you love someone who can't even look at you. Maybe I reminded him of her, whoever she'd been.

There were no photos, no uncles, no aunts, no grandparents. Just me and him. And even if he'd been a worse father, I still would've loved him. It's programmed, that kind of love. Desperate. Like a dog who'll come crawling back even after being kicked away. You can't turn it off. In a way, Dad drinking himself to death was a blessing. It freed me. They came out of their hiding places then, the uncles, the relations, the selfish, uncaring bastards, showed their faces at the damn cheap funeral and I didn't say two words to them. I wondered if I would ever speak to anyone again.

I met Aiden at the graveyard. He was crouched over a plot, tearing out weeds, dirt under his fingernails and a bag of flower bulbs under his arm. He gave me half the flowers, told me I was too pretty to cry and kept saying it until I stopped.

* * *

To start with, I hated every minute of life with Bill. I wanted to kill him. I'd dig my nails hard into his back when he was on top of me, determined to cause him even the most minuscule pain. I bit his mouth, his fingers, his useless dick. He mistook it for passion.

"You fucking love it, don't you?"

His fingers found my clit and rubbed it. Nothing he did could bring me even close to orgasm. I ended up faking it, just so he'd leave me the hell alone. Days stretched into weeks, months, years and life ground on, empty and desperate, sustained only by the hope of Aiden's release.

* * *

I didn't cry.

I never cried.

I cooked the most unappetising food I could imagine. Cauliflowers. Carrots. Bill ate it ravenously. He left money for groceries and housekeeping, a small budget by anyone's standards. But he didn't know me. He didn't know how far I could make a dollar stretch. Potatoes filled out every meal. The cheapest steak from the butcher could taste like fucking filet mignon if you buried it in rock salt a couple hours before grilling.

I walked the extra six blocks to *every cent counts* and got dented cartons of laundry detergent and washing-up liquid for half the regular price. I saved a third of everything he gave me, folded it up and hid it in the one place he'd never look; tampon boxes. They sat at the back of the bathroom cupboard mortifying and unassuming and he never had a goddamn clue.

* * *

Two years after I moved into his house, Bill got promoted to captain. The silver bar on his collar became two. He called them railroad tracks and hated them because he wanted to hit the big time and be a police commander with a fucking silver star. I told him he would be. I bitched with him about his superiors. He told me about all the lowlifes he'd put away, the evidence he'd planted, the goddamn strands of hair and clothing fibres. When he talked about it, his face lit up like goddamn Vegas.

I played the game. I laughed at his jokes, gasped at his intelligence, marvelled at his daring. I kissed him when he left in the morning. When he told me he loved me, I said it back . There was something very detached about it all, like I was scripting my own role in a surreal movie. I had one objective. I could not risk upsetting him. Aiden's life was in his hands. Sometimes, he asked me about him. I told him things I thought were believable.

Summer fling. Teenage mistake.

He seemed to buy it.

"Would you ever want to see him again?" he asked one night. We were in the sitting room, him in his favourite chair, me on the windowsill next to him. The television played a lousy sitcom. Blue played in his cage, testing out the little swing I'd fashioned for him.

"I don't know," I said. "Maybe. But just to see how things have changed, you know? How much better life is now. I couldn't really care less about him, Bill. The one thing I thank him for is bringing us together."

He bought it in the same way he bought everything. I felt his hand on my leg and moved automatically towards him. Sex with him felt almost un-intimate. I could handle it. It was like putting on a pair of shoes you didn't particularly like. Sure, they didn't look good, and didn't feel good but they were necessary for walking. I had to fuck him, keep him happy and pretend it meant the world to me.

He kissed me the way he always kissed me, wet and almost angrily. My hand slipped down over his shirt, tugged at his belt. He pulled back.

"Let's go upstairs. Don't wanna ruin the chair."

***

He loved that fucking armchair. Sometimes Blue would flutter over and sit arrogantly on it like he knew just how much it'd piss Bill off. We had our secrets. One time, the bird came with me when I went grocery shopping. It was both terrifying and exhilarating. Every time I went into a store, he'd wait on a lamppost outside and then fly along behind me. Blue was more than just a bird. He kept me sane.

I bought food, cleaning products, light bulbs, stopped outside the thrift store and considered telling them they were welcome to come over and take Bill's chair. There was a shop next door called NIGHT LIGHT. It sold phones, televisions, cameras, all kinds of electronic equipment. I had twenty spare bucks in my sweaty palm. Blue waited expectantly on top of a mailbox. I glanced around surreptitiously before pushing open the door, my heart thumping as the tall Asian guy behind the counter looked up.

***

I waited.

I didn't know I could wait so long.

I took each day as it came.

I played the game.

Eight long years.

Waiting, faking, baiting, taking.

Hating.

***

They'd moved the pasta at FOOD STOCK. It sat on the top shelf, just out of reach. I stretched up, my fingers brushing the clear plastic packet.

"Hey, let me,"

A hand brushed against mine, picked up the packet and dropped it into my cart. That voice. It went into me, woke something almost dead, something on life support, something that even after all this time had refused to give-the-fuck-up and die. I steadied myself on the edge of the cart and turned around.

"Hey," The word ached out of him. He smiled his one-sided rueful smile. "You can cry now, if you want."

I cried. His arms went around me. I hugged him like I wanted to disappear into him. Sometimes memories become dreams, become fantasies, you wonder if what you remember ever even happened.

He smelled like sweat and warm sand, like himself. I didn't want to let go of him. Tears of relief soaked into his shirt. People forget each other so easily, move on, find new friends, new partners and families and even though I'd always thought we were more than that, a nagging insecurity had planted the idea that perhaps prison would change him. Perhaps I'd never see him again. Perhaps I wasn't biding my time but wasting it.

"You missed me, huh?" His breath warmed the back of my neck.

"So much."

***

His body had filled out. Boy to man. Muscles. Shadowy stubble.

We hadn't even got through Bill's front door when he was on me, his mouth finding mine and claiming it desperately. The keys clattered to the floor. My arms went around him; his hands grasped my ass, tearing my dress up.

"I don't know how I survived," he gasped.

I felt him hard against my stomach, ready as he'd always been. His tongue searched my mouth, fingers already between my legs. I couldn't speak and neither could he. He groaned, dragging off the brand new clothes he wore and pushing me up against the wall so he could kiss me some more. His mouth tasted like relief. Like an eventual oasis after years of staggering through a desert. His lips moved down to my neck, brushing across smooth skin, his tongue leaving a wet path. He pushed his face into my neck and breathed me in like I was a drug. It felt almost too precious.

"He'd visit sometimes," he growled. "Telling me how he fucked you. Lise, it was all I could do not to beat the hell outta him."

My fingers brushed through his soft hair.

"I was waiting," I breathed. "It was nothing."

"I know," he said, but he held me even tighter.

"He doesn't even know how to fuck."

Aiden straightened up. His eyes met mine. "I know."

He knew. He looked at me like he'd always looked at me; like a person looks at a winning lottery ticket. It made me want to tie us together.

I reached up to kiss him again, felt his fingers searching for the zip on my dress. I freed my arms, let the material fall to the floor, my panties following suit. His hands were all over me, his eyes too, his breathing urgent and controlled.

"You look – *feel* – just the same," he murmured. "Like I thought. Like every day *I thought* of you and I'd think 'she'll change. She'll be different. God knows what'll have happened.'" He let out a long breath. "But you're here and you're just the fucking same, Lise. You're like a goddamn dream."

His hands were on my tits, groping roughly, greedily, fingers twisting my nipples until I gasped and almost pulled away. But I didn't. I could never pull away from him. His hands dragged down, one moving to grasp my ass, the other pushing against my snatch. I bit my lip, wetter than I could ever remember being. His fingers weren't gentle. He eased them inside me, one by one, hand pressing against my ass to stop me shrinking back.

"You – feel - *so* - good," he hissed.

His thumb found my clit and he made me come like that first, gave me the first real orgasm I'd had in eight years, leaning against the wall of the living room, his fingers not slowing even as I clenched hard around them. It felt surreal. Hot, sticky, sweet. His thumb pushed against my clit, making me squirm. My hand went out, caught his arm. He didn't stop fingering me.

"You can give me more than one, can't you?"

My mouth opened but no words came out. He touched me deliberately, knowingly, like he had some kind of stored-up memory which detailed exactly how to make me fall apart. "Aiden, *please!*"

I came again, half-sobbing and he moved his hand away

then, grasped my ass and shoved me up against the wall so he could sink his throbbing cock inside me. My wet snatch clenched and quivered around him. His forehead pressed against mine, eyes watching as I sucked in breath after desperate breath. I had to close my eyes when he started moving. Each thrust was defining, purposeful. His cock stretched me deliciously, made me feel so entirely taken. I ground back against him but every time he slammed deep, I was thudded back against the wall.

You don't know love until it feels like it could kill you.

His teeth went into my shoulder as he fucked me, his grunts hoarse and sporadic. We weren't kids anymore but we were the same people. Older. Wiser. More grateful. He fucked me until I felt like there'd be an imprint of my bruised ass in the wall. Even then, I didn't want it to stop. His mouth went from my shoulder to my neck and then up to my cheek, my forehead. Our lips met again. I could taste my sweat on him.

I shuddered through another orgasm and he felt it. His teeth bit hard into my lip, a groan catching in his throat.

"Fuck, Lise. *Fuck!*"

He came violently, still pushing in and out of me as his cock jerked and released.

"Fuck!" His voice sounded like it came from somewhere deeper than his throat. "*Fuck!*"

As raging and urgent as it was, something about it all felt serenely natural. I kissed his gasping mouth until his weight leaned into me and his breathing slowed.

"That was – worth the wait," he eventually breathed.

He released me reluctantly and watched me dress.

"How was prison?" I asked.

He shrugged, locating his clothes and pulling them on. "Free food."

"D'you get beaten up?"

"Not much. Didn't get ass fucked at least." He looked at me. "How 'bout you?"

"Free food," I offered. "Didn't get ass fucked either."

He smiled, eyes drifting around the room, seeing it for the first time. He looked at the birdcage, the armchair, the television, the canary watching him from the windowsill.

"We should get outta here," he said. "If that cop came in he'd put us away forever."

I smiled.

"One minute."

He watched as I stood haphazardly on a chair in the corner, digging out the small video camera secreted inside the alarm sensor.

"What the fuck?"

I jumped off the chair and pressed the camera into his hand.

"Don't lose it. It's all we have on him."

He followed me wordlessly to the bathroom and watched as I gathered tampon boxes out of the cupboard.

"Uh, Lise? Tampons haven't been discontinued, you know. If you wanna steal something, steal something valuable."

"It's not fucking tampons. It's money."

I showed him the contents of a box.

"Oh. Okay."

"It'll tide us over a while, right?"

"Right," he said, very softly.
He found a small plastic bag and I dropped the boxes into it. He carefully pocketed the camera. Blue watched us prepare to leave. I looked at him. It was almost six. He fluttered over to the cage and then to the window, hesitating just a second before taking off.

"I never dug up that money you told me about," I mused, heading for the door. "D'you wanna go get it?"

Aiden smiled.

"No. It's not raining anymore, is it?"

Made in London

She could feel him watching her but every time her eyes flicked to catch his, he'd be looking down at the tattered day-worn Metro in his hand. Even from ten metres away, the paper looked scuffed and dirty, and it'd been folded in half since the man had first picked it up.

They'd both boarded the train at Liverpool Street with the late-commute crowd. 18:27. Two strangers in a crowd of dozens more. A wet night. The air outside had been fresh and damp, an earlier thunderstorm having faded into a typical London drizzle.

Winter. Glowing yellow-white streetlights. Car headlights and pattering rain. Smoke misting from exhausts. The kind of scene that'd look cosy in pictures or on Christmas cards. But it didn't feel cosy when you were running along the dirty streets, car horns in your ears and rain chasing you down the stairs into the hollow commotion of the underground station.

Ella sighed, still content to have caught the train, and leaned against the metal pole beside her. She tucked a loose strand of damp hair behind her ear and glanced at the man again. Still reading the Metro, apparently. The train had already made four stops, handfuls of commuters trudging from the carriage off into the night. And this man apparently hadn't read more than half the sports page.

Ella wondered. She shrugged in her head and turned her attention back to her phone. And two seconds later he was looking at her again. She knew it without even checking. She felt it like a person feels the weather. Not a sixth sense. More tangible than that. More obvious. Like the first elusive notes on a radio betraying the warmth of an entire song. Something. Ella frowned at her phone, resisting the urge to try and catch him in the act again. He'd be too quick and then maybe he'd assume she might be interested.

Distractedly, she blinked at the screen of her phone. Small bold news headlines glared at her accusingly. Wars. Bombs. Murders. Ella let out a breath. Don't think about it. She swallowed and her throat was so dry it hurt. Ironic. Dehydrated on the wettest night of the year. She almost smiled but caught herself.

She chanced a look at the stranger again. He seemed totally focused on his newspaper. But he still hadn't unfolded it. A damp satchel hung from one of his broad shoulders and she could see the cap of a water bottle poking out from inside. Her throat clenched a little. How could she have gotten so thirsty without realising?

Her eyes went back up his arm and to his face. He looked up then. Made eye contact and didn't break it. But he didn't smile. He just looked at her in the most physical way one person can ever look at another. It felt violent. For a few long seconds, the shock prevented her reacting. And then heat surged. Anger? Embarrassment? Why should she be embarrassed?

She tore her eyes away and busied herself with searching through her bag for water she knew wouldn't be there. Her pulse raced and, for a while, she couldn't hear anything else. Did he want sex? The idea seemed implausible. Commuters had a silent, unspoken code of conduct but then, he didn't look like a regular. And she'd never seen him before. She'd definitely have remembered a man like him. Tall. Check. Handsome. Double check. His eyelashes looked like they were an inch long, even from such a distance.

Ella rolled her eyes inwardly. It didn't matter. It wouldn't happen. She abandoned the water search and glared at her reflection in the train door. Sex. No time. Never any time. Not now. Not ever. Life. This life. Something she'd been instrumental in creating. How could she have let it happen?

Every little thing had stacked up into a teetering pile and it seemed like one small imbalance could make it all fall apart. Too tired. Way too tired. Too much running around, chasing elevators, killing time at the photocopier, filing and fetching and coffee and lunch orders and reapplying lipstick and killing herself with her own bright white chirpy telephone voice.

And his eyes were on her again, and she knew it and he knew she knew it and he looked at her like he wanted to fuck her. Oh god. Was she getting ahead of herself? Did he want her? How could he?

Everything that could happen and everything that couldn't happen. And it could. It wouldn't take very much. Catch his eye. Walk over. Ask him what the hell he wants. She had the words in her mind, but they were in disarray, unable to form a logical sentence. You. What. Why. Fuck. Fuck. Because maybe it'd all be a misunderstanding. Maybe he'd mistaken her for someone else or maybe he was looking at her the way people look at things in the distance; looking but not seeing; just a point where a person's eyes rest so their mind can get on with whatever the hell it needs to get on with.

But it wasn't that kind of look. She knew it. He knew it. And she couldn't do anything about it. Just a man. A stranger. Jeans and a t-shirt and rain wet hair. And six stops until her station. It seemed like the journey would take forever. Maybe he'd leave first. She didn't know. She couldn't tell. The way he stood seemed so comfortable and yet so unimportant like he wouldn't make a sound if he walked away.

The sentences began to form.

What are you looking at? (Too childish.)

"Is there something I can help you with? (Too whorish.)

What's your problem? (Too confrontational.)

Ella blew out a breath. Fuck it. Just fuck everything. It didn't matter. None of it mattered. All she'd wanted all afternoon was to get home, shut the door, slide the bolt across, spend half an hour under a hot shower and then eat popcorn, ice-cream and whatever the hell else she'd saved up for a day like this. At least, that had been the plan. But now there was another part to the equation making it so much harder to figure out. The way he looked at her.

He was doing it again and she didn't acknowledge it but she felt it and her stomach almost hurt. Some kind of hungering appreciation. Nobody had ever looked at her quite that way. Nobody. Not even the guys she'd been naked with. There'd been a sick futility to all her relationships. Doing things for the sake of doing them. Just another part of the weekly routine. Like work. Like eating.

And this man who'd never touched her, never spoken to her, never even been in the same room as her, was looking at her in a way that made her feel so wanted it was dirty. A kind of desperate reverence. He wanted to fuck her. It was an assumption and yet it was so obvious she felt people might laugh if she'd denied it. But what people? The crowd on the train had no idea. They didn't see her and they didn't see him. Absorbed in phones, in books, in music, in their own heads.

It suddenly felt like she saw them for the very first time. Like she'd been one of them only yesterday and now something had dragged her out of that dream and this was real-life, glaring and obvious and it'd never been something she'd ever thought of as beautiful but it seemed that way now.

He looked at her as she looked at everyone else and she wondered why. Why her? Exactly why? Why is anyone more important than anyone else? Beauty isn't the way a thing looks but the way you see it and why was he seeing her and did it even matter? Shouldn't she just accept that he was?

She forced herself to look at him. Not at his face because she knew she didn't have any hope of holding eye contact. His dark t-shirt. His arms. The kind of arms one might feel safe in. Ella blew out a breath and fought the urge to hate herself. Her eyes dropped to the front of his jeans. His cock. Was that a more reasonable thing to think about?

The train stopped again. Passengers exited. Marble Arch

. Three stops until Notting Hill. And then what? She'd get off. Chances were, he wouldn't. And this was all it was ever going to be. Some wordless, pointless connection on the Central line. Unless. Well. Unless she made it into something more. She considered it whilst knowing she didn't have the nerve. She thought of his cock again, trying to imagine it with nothing to go on. Thoughts were harmless, after all. Nobody would ever know what was going on inside her crazy mind.

His eyes were still on her. She turned her back on him, ejected thoughts of his anatomy from her mind and tried to remember which flavour ice-cream waited patiently in her freezer. The train drew to another stop. People moved, leaving and boarding, jostling past. She glanced back at where the stranger had been standing. He'd disappeared. But there was a sudden presence right behind her. Not touching, though if she took a step back, they'd have made contact. Close enough to feel without feeling.

She didn't turn around. She looked to her side, saw the edge of his bag. She almost panicked. But what was there to panic about? His hand had curled around the metal pole a foot above hers. Clean nails. Strong fingers. Before she knew what she was doing, she was imagining them inside her. The thought almost made her legs give way.
He didn't speak. He didn't touch her. He just stood behind her. Maybe he was waiting for her to do something. Ella thought about all the possible things she could do until her station came and then she got off without doing a single one of them and hurried home.

* * *

Nothing had changed, she told herself as she lay wide-awake in bed that night. It was all in her head. A muted connection. Eighteen minutes of her life. Nothing. Trivial. And yet, he was all she could think of. Why couldn't she have at least asked his name? She could have bumped into him accidentally-on purpose and struck up a conversation. But she hadn't. She'd done nothing but be woefully passive and chances were, she'd never see him again.

She wondered about him. His job. Where he lived. What was in his bag? Whether he looked at other girls the way he looked at her. And then back to the safer questions. Did he smoke? Did he have a sense of humour?

There'd been a time where that kind of lonely-hearts-ad thing had been important to her. Stupidly important since none of it seemed to matter anymore. None of the guys she'd been with had impacted her life in a good way. They'd merely added cynicism and workaholicism and a distrust of all their kind.

Men. Inflated egos over fragile insecurities. Ulterior motives and indecisive immaturity. Not worth the time. Not worth the free drinks. And yet, a stranger making eyes at her on a train suddenly seemed more worthwhile? Ella wanted to laugh at herself but feared she might start crying.

"What the hell is going on with you?" she asked and immediately felt foolish for talking out loud in an empty flat.

She tried not to think of the way he'd looked at her. It felt like too much all at once. Too dangerous. Too obvious. It made her stomach clench in the most wistful way. She could have fucked him. She could have made it happen somehow. And even though she'd never been the kind of person who'd even entertained the idea of casual sex, she found herself full of regrets.

Everything felt hot.

Her fingers pushed up the hem of her t-shirt and walked across her stomach deliberatively. She thought of him. Not so much the way he looked but the way he stood so close to her, maybe a foot between them. Twelve inches of patient distance. And it affected her so intensely. It made her heart pound and her eyes close.

What would she have done if he'd touched her? Let him? Or shoved him away? It wasn't the kind of thing you could speculate about.

But there were other things. Her hand slipped beneath the waistband of her underwear and stroked tentatively. She couldn't remember feeling so turned on. Her legs shifted apart without instruction and her fingertip pressed hard against her clit, making her whole body ache.

"Fuck," She whispered the word almost desperately.
In her mind, he was already hers. He was all hers and naked and beautiful and hard and gentle all at once. How would he fuck? Her mind flickered like some crazy porno, all the best scenes she'd ever watched spliced together into one intensely satisfying reel. And it was stupid. She knew it was utterly ridiculous to think all these things about a man she'd never see again but what was the harm?

Her fingers slicked back and forth shamelessly. She'd never been wetter. Her shirt was already soaked with sweat and her teeth bit hard on her bottom lip. She imagined him recklessly; the way he'd feel, the way he'd touch her, his fingers. God, why did the thought of his fingers make her so breathless?

Her free hand grasped her tit through the damp t-shirt. It hurt in the best way. She thought of his cock again, imagined it in his hand, rubbing against her face. One of her ex's had been seriously into that kind of thing but his fixation had made it almost tiresome. In her mind, if the stranger on the train jerked off in her face, nothing could be hotter.

Memories and fantasies pieced together, the bad seamlessly edited out until she got so close, she had to pull her hand away. The bedroom window was cracked open and the rain had picked up speed again. All of a sudden, she realised she remembered how the stranger had smelled when he stood behind her.

Like rain. And pine. And grass. She laughed a little, more at herself than anything and pushed her face into the pillow, turning onto her front as her hand pressed against her throbbing snatch. She blew out a breath. The way he looked at her. It all came down to that look. Those eyes. She didn't even know what colour they were but did it matter when she felt them inside her so completely?

He wanted to fuck her. He wanted her. She didn't know anything about him but the thought filled her with swooping warmth. Her finger pressed against her clit and she moaned into her pillow, lifting her hips off the mattress to give her hand better access.

His cock. She thought of how it would feel in her hand, solid and warm and throbbing. If she could make him come that way or if he'd prefer to push it inside her. Her teeth sank into the pillow. Her eyes were closed tight. If she stretched hard enough, she could practically feel him. It spiralled out of control suddenly; before she'd fully thought of it, she was imagining his voice in her ear, his weight against hers, the way he'd hold her and make her come. The things he'd make her do.

The thoughts spun and twisted into one another, building steadily, almost out of her control. Her mind raced. All of it came back to that look. Everything centred on it. He wanted her. Was he thinking of her? The idea sent a thrilling shock through her. Was he? Somewhere, anywhere in the rainy, dark city was he thinking of her like she was thinking of him? Was he touching himself? Fuck.

She came quicker than she'd wanted, pressing urgently against her own hand as she gasped into the soft pillow, her entire body soaked in sweat. It went on, desperate and draining until she finally slumped down onto the bed. She tucked her knees up to her chest and huddled there, trying to catch her breath
Fantasies were fantasies. Based on books and music and movies. Things she bought and believed in if only to dream. Maybe he was nothing like she envisioned. How could he be? But did it matter when he looked at her the way he did? How could one look fill her with so much clenching warmth?

She fell asleep with a lilting thought that maybe no one would ever look at her that way again and maybe for that reason, nobody would ever be good enough.

* * *

It came around again almost as though to taunt her. As though to say, "You wished you'd had the nerve to do something about him so here's your chance,

" What were the chances? Two times in two days. The same train. Almost all the same people. And he stood there, the newspaper unfolded this time, blue jeans instead of black but everything else was exactly the same.

Ella eyed him surreptitiously, aching with tension. There was simply no way she could not talk to him. And yet, her feet refused to move. Her fist was tight around the safety pole. She thought of all the things that could go wrong. There weren't very many, or perhaps she deliberately wasn't thinking hard enough. She thought of her life, of days stretching meaninglessly into one another. She thought of never seeing him again, of speculating endlessly for weeks to come

. The train hissed into the second station. He looked up, looked right at her and smiled. She started towards him. Maybe he'd have a horrible voice. Maybe he didn't even speak the same language. Maybe when he opened his mouth the fantasy would fade into the nothingness of two days ago. Real life always revealed the ugly side of dreams. She tried to prepare for disappointment but jittering hope encompassed everything and the closer she got to him, the faster her mind raced. Everything hinged on this moment; this very moment; just a girl on a nondescript train moving towards a stranger.

She reached him at last. He hadn't stopped looking at her the whole time.

Up close, there was more. Maybe a couple years older than

she'd thought. More stubble. An un-utilised ear piercing. His eyes were blue-green.

"Hi," she said.

He smiled.

"I was hoping you'd come over," he replied and his voice was so deep and warm that on the cold, dark night, everything suddenly glowed gold.

Unfamiliar

Silvia exhaled a long breath as she pulled out of the Wilson Building parking lot. It had been a long day, on top of four other long days and she looked forward to the weekend. Her purse sat on the passenger seat and she fumbled through it for a much-needed cigarette. Lighting up, she let the window down a couple of inches and relaxed into the drive. She lived a good hour from the office and the journey home often felt like the only real time she had to think.

The cool wind purred in through the open window and she sucked hard on her cigarette, smoking it down to the butt before she'd even begun to enjoy it. She reached automatically for another and putting it between her lips, lit it singlehandedly. The roads were largely empty, partly due to the late hour. The car drove powerfully, and comfortably too. Lately, it seemed like a friend, a confidante almost.

She pulled to a stop at a light and tapped ash out of the window. Across the wide road she could see a string of bars and restaurants, people laughing, careless, happy. It felt so far away, like a dream, almost a movie.

A vehicle pulled up in the lane beside her at the red light, music and smoke coming out of the windows. She couldn't help glancing at the driver. He looked too tall for even his truck. One tattooed, muscular arm rested where the window disappeared into the car door. He caught her looking and winked. She gave him a tight smile and turned her attention back to the road, already blushing. God. *You're a psychiatrist*, she reminded herself. *A highly regarded professional.*

Someone else, someone young, uninhibited and beautiful would probably give that guy a good time before the night was through.

Silvia flipped down the sun visor and looked at her wide green eyes in the mirror. There were little lines at the corners.

Fuck. She snapped the visor back up in disgust and tapped her manicured nails on the steering wheel, impatient for the light to change. She could feel the tattooed guy in the next car still looking at her. It would be easy, right? Turn, smile at him, drive somewhere, or maybe not drive. Maybe just pull up to the side of the road, get out of the goddamn Range Rover and climb into his dirty truck and let him fuck her whichever nasty way he liked.

She almost seriously considered it. But then, common sense prevailed. No condoms. She almost laughed. Condoms hadn't bothered her for years, but that dated back to when she'd used the pill. A long time ago now. University. Private clients. More than one sometimes.

Silvia sucked in a long, wistful breath. *Youth is wasted on the young.* Not that she qualified as old. Not yet. Not even thirty-five. Inside, she still felt young, and some days thought she might still be playing dress-up in her mother's clothes. Pretending to be something different. Saying the right things. Believing something else. How much had she really changed?

The red light faded, the green appeared. She shifted the car into gear, raised the clutch and felt that familiar, gentle purr as it came to life. JESUS. Everything felt sexual to her these days, and Ronan hadn't helped. Could he be the worst? When he'd talk about his meaningless sexual connections, she felt almost like a voyeur. It turned her on, and she knew it turned *him* on to make her uncomfortable.

They turned each other on. Surely, it couldn't be a useful form of therapy. But she could hardly tell him to stop talking. Her job as a goddamn psychiatrist made her duty bound to listen to perverts like Ronan. *Perverts.* Silvia smirked. Like she could talk. The sessions had stirred up tensions inside her that she'd thought were long gone. In her locked desk drawer back in her office, she'd had to dig out her emergency change of panties, so rattled she'd been by Ronan's story of the receptionist he'd fucked en route to the locked offices of a corrupt *FTSE 100 cfo.*

"I mean, she was practically asking for it," he'd said in that easy, almost dreamlike tone. "As if she knew the score. Sometimes I wonder why these girls aren't better utilised. I mean, a *receptionist.* She saw through me better than any of the suits. But then, maybe it was a purely sexual understanding. Just fucking." His eyes closed momentarily and he shook his head. "Meaningless but satisfying. You know?"

Silvia had blinked, temporarily caught off guard. Ronan smiled, like he knew the exact effect of his words. Maybe he did know. After all, his job entailed finding out the things people wanted to keep hidden. *Perhaps he knew about her past*, she thought and as indifferent as she tried to be about it, she couldn't help cringing at the idea.

Ten years ago. She'd had less sex in those ten years than she'd had in a week back in the university days. Over and over. Reckless and hedonistic. Funnily enough, she didn't regret it very much. She looked back at those days with a half-smile, almost jealous of her younger self. Some days, she'd even drive someplace, somewhere far away, to some bar or club where the rich and kinky congregated.

But things had changed. The men didn't dazzle her in the way they had when she'd been younger. After all, now she knew them too well. She read them too easily. And yet, the hunger didn't wane. She'd find herself home again, watching some awful porn scene and unable to stop the raw pleasure it provided. The word *hypocrite* came to mind. A psychiatrist. Working for the secret service. Watching porn.

Sex addiction didn't qualify as a regular form of addiction like alcoholism or drug use. You couldn't clear desire out of your body like a chemical. And even if you thought you had, it always managed to prove you wrong. Weeks, months, even years down the line it would re-emerge. *Hey. Remember me? You thought you'd gotten rid of me. Well, you failed. I'm here to fucking stay.* Repression seemed to be the only real way to stay out of trouble but who in their right mind thought THAT had ever worked?

The agents had been getting to her. Guys without real lives but with real urges and dependencies. Doctor-patient confidentiality. It existed. After all, their conversations were personal; were some way of figuring out the importance of what featured in their espionage-riddled minds. Most of them didn't really need her. They could have talked to a wall. After all, they were smart enough.

But they still came. Therapy didn't count as compulsory but the oft-mocked HR department highly recommended it. The agents who needed the most help didn't come. And honestly, Silvia felt relieved. In a way, she feared them. They were so entrenched in their own minds, such lone, introverted souls; after all the calculating and double-crossing, she sometimes wondered whether they even knew themselves.

Don't get attached. Easier said than done. How can anyone really be emotionless, be detached, cool and unaffected when men are telling you about the people they've killed? They all had blood on their hands. After all, there's something good in everyone and when a life is prematurely taken, you take away that hope for change, for that goodness to grow and blossom into something that could kill everything that came before. Is it true? Or are some people too far gone? Silvia sighed. Questions without answers, from the doctor who should have had all the answers.

Sometimes, she wondered if the agents could see through her. After all, they were shrewd people. The most intelligent in the country, the authorities would have you believe. They noticed things. They noticed everything. And then they would almost audibly deconstruct things in their minds, figuring out what counted as innocent and what could have another meaning.

It must have been exhausting, Silvia often thought when she'd see their eyes periodically sweep the interior of her office. She'd had one man who'd go over to the window every five minutes and peer out. OCD? Or an army-routine mentality? And then she had Ronan. A goddamn enigma. He sat on the couch for a start. Everyone saw the couch as a cliché; a compulsory fake-comfortable piece of furniture in counsellors offices the world over. Most agents would take the chair opposite her or opt for an armchair.

But Ronan would drop onto the couch, smile that easy smile, and look pointedly at the coffee machine in the corner. He'd been in, earlier. Silvia didn't make the coffee. She buzzed in Evelyn, her secretary, not shifting her attention from Ronan.

He always seemed to be up to something and she didn't quite dare to turn her back on him.

Evelyn had made the steaming coffee while Ronan and Silvia had watched each other; him blatantly and her surreptitiously. He never talked when someone else appeared in the room. And he always used up his full hour. If a disturbance occurred, he added on the lost minutes. A perfectionist? Or did he just enjoy himself? He even took time off from field work to see her. Her. Silvia Hill. The shrink. She never felt like a psychiatrist during his appointments.

Don't psychoanalyse yourself. It's work, for fuck's sake.

Hot coffee. Poor Evelyn couldn't stand the silence. She chattered away about the weather, so helplessly British and yet, so enviable in her own way. Young and carefree. She had a family. A fiancé, too. Silvia had even been invited to the wedding though she knew she wouldn't go. Ronan didn't acknowledge Evelyn's presence, didn't look at her, didn't even thank her for the coffee, or for the shortbread she'd fetched especially from the kitchen on the floor above. RUDE BASTARD. Silvia found herself being over-appreciative as if to make up for it.

"Thanks, Evelyn. That's wonderful. I can never make it so fast. Thanks for all your help. Don't you want some? At your desk? No? Okay. Thanks again. Watch the carpet; it's frayed at the door. Thank you so much."

Ronan had watched, silently, a ghost of a smirk hiding behind his polite smile. He'd waited for Evelyn to leave before he'd leaned forward and picked up his coffee. He'd inhaled the steam for a second and then sipped.

"Not bad."

Silvia had tried to smile.

"So. How are you, Ronan?"

Feigned formality. Why pretend to be doctor and patient when they were the only two people in the room?

Silvia tried not to think about him. Work-life balance. Maybe she ought to call her parents. Do something normal. Jesus. She reached forward and jabbed the 'on' button of the radio. The xx were playing. She almost turned it off but the song caught her too fast and her hand dropped back onto the gear stick. Music. Manufactured money-making melodies. Musicians were such attention seekers, she thought, but still didn't turn the radio off and instead found herself turning up the volume.

Ronan Carter. She knew his name, his date of birth, his correspondence address and even a residential one. He had a national insurance number, a telephone number, a passport number but everything bar his name had been changed multiple times in her file alone. Did it matter? People were people, despite all the controls and restrictions and tracking mechanisms. He hadn't changed from the man who'd maintain eye contact even when talking about the lewdest things. She'd never met anyone like him.

***

The parking lot seemed crowded when Silvia pulled in And her appointed space had been occupied by a flashy red Jaguar. She considered blocking the offender in but instead parked on the street. For a while, she didn't get out of the car. It felt wonderfully silent. Peaceful. A dog-walker passed by, then a jogger wearing a high-visibility vest. Silvia picked up her bag and work shoes, exited the car and headed towards her apartment building.

She lived on the fourth floor and as she approached the building, she frowned. A light seemed to be on in her apartment. She could see the yellow glow. The living space. The blinds weren't closed. Had she left a light on? Or had a burglar with no sense of timing decided to target her?

You left the light on, she told herself as she stepped into the elevator. *It's winter. Mornings are dark. You put the light on when you were making breakfast and you forgot to turn it off.* Even as she said the words to herself, she knew they didn't make sense. Silvia Hill did *not* forget to turn off lights. Ever.

But she had to tell herself she had, because why else would she be walking so confidently out of the elevator? If a burglar or robber or murderer had decided to visit her, she should be calling the police. But she didn't. She didn't know why not. For a few seconds, she had visions of the newspaper headlines. *Doctor killed in own home. Single white female: murdered.*

"For fuck's sake," she said aloud and the sound of her own voice steadied her a little. She put her key in the lock and turned it. The door opened unceremoniously and she walked in. The hall appeared dark but light from the next open door beamed in. She closed the front door and walked into the living area. She stopped short. Ronan stood there. Ronan Carter. At ten o'clock. In her goddamn apartment.

"Nice shoes," he said, eying her Nikes. "Can't drive in heels?"

His elbow rested on the mantelpiece. For a few seconds, Silvia didn't – *couldn't* – speak. She set down her things, doing her best to maintain a poker face while her mind raced. *It's okay. You can deal with him. You're a fucking therapist. You're his therapist. Just – stay fucking calm. Fuck!*

She tried not to notice how attractive he looked.

"Ronan, what are you doing here?"

He smiled. "I'm not entirely sure."

"Is everything okay?"

He looked at her hard.

"Nothing's ever okay. You know that."

Silvia felt out of place in her own apartment. The top two buttons of his shirt were undone and his jacket lay on the arm of the sofa. An empty water glass sat on the coffee table. At least he'd used a coaster.

"Is the Jaguar yours?" she asked.

He frowned. "The what?"

"The car. In my spot."

"No. I got a cab. Why?"

"I – I don't know," Silvia shook her head. "Look, what do you want? What are you here for, Ronan?"

He blew out a breath.

"Company. Someone real."

She didn't want to believe him. "But me? Why?"

"It's new," he shrugged his broad shoulders. "You're new."
"Not really," Silvia frowned. After all, she'd known him for two years.

"I mean *different*," he clarified. "From everything else. You're – real, maybe. Not a mirror, not smoke, not pretending. I was okay before you came along and replaced the old doctor. He was grey. He was easy. But you make me – impatient. I think a lot about the one hour a week we get to talk. I don't know, Silver. Maybe it was better before you came along. Just existing."

"It's Silvia," she managed to say. "And you should call me Doctor Hill."

He smiled, a genuine, contagious smile.

"Y'see? How can I not – how can I not LIVE when you talk to me like that?"

Silvia swallowed hard, fighting for a rational argument. "I think you're reading too much into moments," she finally said.

"Moments?" He raised an eyebrow.

"Yes. Sometimes we focus on something small, inconsequential, like the way a musician sings a particular word. It doesn't mean very much to anything at all but we obsess over it. And that's okay. But not for a long period of time."

Even as she said the words, they seemed to apply so perfectly to his arched eyebrow. That one, tiny movement did crazy things to her. She needed him to LEAVE.
"You're not a word in a song," Ronan said resolutely.
Silvia almost rolled her eyes.

She said, "So what am I? A human. You've met thousands." He watched her walk across the room. She picked up a glass water bottle from the sideboard and drank a good half of it, leaning against the wall.

"And I've read them all," Ronan said. "You know, Silver, I wouldn't be here if this was something small. We're smart people. Maybe I'm doing myself a disservice. This isn't good, is it? Coming to your apartment? It makes me look – weak, maybe. Needy."

His self-assessment made her soften a little.

"I've never thought of you as weak," she said mildly.

He laughed.

"Because I'm a machine. I've been this way since I got out of school. Civil Service job. I just – at first it seemed wonderful."

He shook his head, half-smiling. "Unconventional. I felt like I was special. And then like some kind of esteemed vigilante. Like a comic book adventure."

"What's changed?" Silvia asked.

"My age," he replied, though it didn't seem like he believed it. "Or maybe I just need more from life."

"What do you need, Ronan?"

He smiled when she said his name.

"I need – to be honest. With someone. I don't know how much longer I want to hide behind the scenes of life. I want to be a part of it."

"You can be," Silvia said encouragingly. "There's no reason why you can't date. You know the protocol; you know how much you can say."

"But what if I want to say more?" His eyes met hers. "What if I want to be brutally honest?"

"You've managed to hold it in for almost twenty years. I don't see the problem."

He frowned. "Yes, you do. Me and you, we're the same. You know how to keep a secret."

Silvia smiled. "No. We are – *very* – different."

He didn't smile. His eyes narrowed as though she'd offended him. For a second, it seemed like he might walk towards her. He didn't. He paced towards the door, stopped

, tilted his head to the side and surveyed her.

"Are we?" he asked, quietly. "Don't we crave the same things? Doesn't it sicken you to see how easy other people have it? Aren't you jealous of their freedom, of how totally unrepressed they are?"

Silvia blinked. Did he know? Maybe he knew. Maybe he'd been that far back. Fucking BASTARD. He knew her address. He stood inside her apartment, for God's sake! He'd taken the time to figure it out. He knew. He knew everything.

"I know what you do," he said, his voice even quieter now. "Where you go. What you look for. And yet you can't find it, can you? It's the same with me. Each one is just a – I don't know. A means to an end." He looked at her hard. "Can we not – just - can't we?"

"Can't we WHAT, Ronan?" Silvia snapped. "FUCK? Is that what you want? Is that what you're here for?"
His mask slipped. She saw the danger, felt the need, the impatience.

"I just," It sounded like it hurt for him to speak. An ache undercut his voice. "I just want – something more. There should be more. You know? Afterwards? More than emptiness?"

"Ronan, I-"

"Don't say my name," he interrupted. "It only makes it worse."

Silvia wanted to hug him. She wanted to put her arms

around him and hold him as if that could somehow make everything work out. For a few seconds she could ignore the sex; and could see him as a human, as a lost, washed-up, worn-out human. Somewhere inside the facade, inside the polished intelligence, he mirrored the way she felt.

But there were lines. There were boundaries, repercussions, consequences. Doctor Hill. How could she be expected to be responsible for a grown man? How could anyone expect her to send him away? The connection felt too deep, felt already inappropriate in the most human of ways. She didn't usually get further than shallow issues. Easy things. And this had become far too deep, deeper than her goddamn conversations with family, for fuck's sake! She'd never felt so attuned to anyone before. A sense of surrealism came over her. She couldn't figure out whether it felt good or bad.

"Ronan, you should go. Maybe you need some rest."

"I really don't," he said, his voice hard.

It felt as though they were on the brink of something dangerous and addictive. Silvia found her mind flickering back to her first cigarette.

"You want to throw me out?" Ronan leaned his weight against the door. "Go ahead. But don't forget that I know you, Silver. The service doesn't worry much about doctors, does it? Wouldn't it be a shock if everyone knew what you were really like? D'you remember what you were doing New Year's Eve fifteen years ago? Or should I say WHO you were doing? How many were there?"

Silvia's smile felt more like a grimace.

"Blackmail? Is that what you're going to stoop to? Field games?"

He didn't smile.

"Call it what you want. Obviously you need something to take away the responsibility. Here I am, coercing you, blackmailing you, dredging up the past. Fuck, Silver!" He ran his hands through his hair, walking towards her. "It's all me, okay? Is that what you need? Blame it on me. I'll take it. I'm the bad guy, I'm the one who fucking came over, this is all me. You're just – powerless. Does that help? Does that make it okay for you?"

"You think you're so goddamn intelligent," Silvia wished she didn't have her back to the wall. It took away the chance of escape.
"I AM intelligent," Ronan said. His words weren't arrogant; they were simply stating a fact. "But I'm also just a man. And you look pretty and you smell addictive and for some reason, something about you just... sticks."

He'd been physically closer to her before but the space between them had never felt so charged and alive.

"You know, I got in the cab and the driver asked where I wanted to go," His voice came out as little more than a growl.

"And I hadn't even planned it. I just heard myself giving your address."

His hand came out, warm and strong as it curled around the side of her neck. Silvia tried not to lean into it. A part of her still felt caught off-guard. She really didn't have any idea what he might do. He stepped closer. She had to tilt her chin up to keep his face in view. Her hands were fidgeting at her sides like they wanted to push him back, create some distance, but she didn't quite dare.

He kissed her very softly, his lips barely grazing hers, as though he were testing how far she'd let him get. Then he kissed her a little harder. Silvia didn't stop him. She knew she should. In the back of her mind, a very sensible and refined voice kept reiterating that this encounter would screw things up at work; it would never be the same again. But things weren't great anyway, were they? Ronan always managed to make her feel uncomfortable. How much worse could it get? Besides, his mouth on hers didn't feel wrong in the slightest. It had been so long since anyone had touched her. Part of her wanted to pull away. His gentleness had a violence to it, as though it might be a front to something deeper and crueller. It didn't seem right that he would be so hesitant and receptive.

She found herself thinking of David Attenborough documentaries, where predators would move so slowly and sleekly before seizing the moment to decimate their prey.

Were humans really much more than animals? It became too hard to think, to second-guess, to even try protesting.

She felt his hands around her wrists, pinning them to the wall, his mouth moving down across her neck. She tried to move and his grip tightened instinctively. He wouldn't let go. Not now. Not now, when he'd gotten so far, when his knee pushed between her legs and she had nowhere to run.

"Isn't it nice?" Ronan murmured against her skin. "To be where we should have been all along?"

Silvia didn't say anything. She told herself coldly that the option of stopping him still existed. Just a word. One word. She even opened her mouth. But then Ronan kissed her again, his tongue inside her mouth this time and it felt so intimate and fulfilling that she couldn't do anything. He knew he'd got inside, figured out the locks on the doors and had nothing left to do but run wild. Silvia felt it coming, felt the way his body seemed to tense and prepare. Little things.

He pulled back and his hands dropped hers, moving instead to her waist and spinning her around to face the wall. Then his hands were on her hips, pulling her back into him. She flattened her hands against the wall instinctively and his body pushed against hers, grinding hard.

"Fuck," he breathed. His hand grasped her braid, tugging her head back so he could kiss her neck again, only this time his mouth had become wetter, hungrier, more abandoned. For the first time, Silvia became aware of the heat between her legs and she found herself pushing back against his hard cock. It had been too long. Far too long.

"You want this?" Ronan's voice sounded hoarse. "You fucking want this, Silver?"

His hands tugged her blouse free from the waistband of her skirt and then his fingers were venturing beneath, darting up the flat of her stomach to push into her bra. His hands were cool against her skin but the discomfort became nothing when his fingers found her nipples and tugged hard.

"Ronan, please,"

His fingers didn't move.

"What did I tell you about saying my name?" he breathed. "It makes me even – worse."

Silvia's teeth bit down on her lip as he pushed harder against her. She could feel his cock against her ass, the hard, trapped length lying in wait beneath layers of clothing. His mouth moved roughly, sucking and biting her neck, his hand moving to try and free her shoulder from her blouse.

"Take it off," he finally growled.

Silvia didn't think twice. She pressed her forehead against the wall, so she could use her hands to shakily unbutton her blouse. Still grinding against her, he helped her drag the shirt off, before making quick work of her bra. Then his hands were all over her, groping possessively, fingertips dragging over every inch of her exposed torso. Her eyes closed tight. It had been too long, way too long, waiting for something that she'd pretended she didn't need. Somewhere in the back of her mind had been that grainy idea that maybe the eventual give wouldn't be worth it.

She'd been wrong. Ronan's touch had ceased to be gentle; he'd become rough and grasping, thumbs digging between her ribs, his fingers grappling like he wanted to take something out of her. And all the while, she could feel his hard cock grinding against her ass, his mouth moving along the curve between her neck and shoulder. His hand slipped down, caught the fastening on her skirt and tugged it free, before unzipping it.

Silvia straightened up, pushing him back as she stripped out of the rest of her clothes, hearing him follow suit behind her. She turned to face him and he pushed her back against the wall, his hand sliding between their bodies and finding her snatch. Her breath came out in a shudder and as if he knew how much it got to her, he groaned.

"It's never like this," He sounded pained. "Never, Silver. You're so fucking – perfect."

She felt his fingers move purposefully, knowingly and loved how unfamiliar they felt; so much bigger than her own. Instinct told her to pull away, but the more she let him touch her, the better it felt. She knew he could feel just how wet she'd become and something about him knowing made her feel as though she couldn't hide anything from him. His fingers slicked back and forth gently at first as though warming up, before he found her clit and stroked it so sublimely that her mouth fell open.

"Fuck," she breathed. "Fuck!"

His eyes were on her, drinking in every move she made and at her exclamation his face broke into a smile.

"You're so goddamn pretty."
He caught her clit between his thumb and forefinger – she didn't know how he managed it, considering how wet she'd become – driving her closer to a rushing orgasm. She couldn't speak, couldn't think; could only push back against his hand, gasping pitifully.

"I love that fucking noise," Ronan hissed. His hand curled around her snatch and he kissed her on the mouth, his tongue almost down her throat. It felt unfamiliar, and yet starkly real.

No more backtracking. No more sitting in the goddamn car

outside bars, watching men she'd never fuck. No more sitting across from him in the office and having to cross her legs to stop squirming.

She felt his hand grasp her arm, moving her effortlessly. Then they were falling back onto her sofa, him on top, a forgotten magazine pressing against her shoulder. Ronan pulled it free, tossed it onto the floor, his mouth still on hers. She felt like she ought to take a breath but why bother when his kiss felt like it might be all she'd ever need to survive? Her hand fought its way down their bodies, desperate to touch him. She had to push him up a little to get to where she wanted but he still didn't break the kiss, his teeth sinking into her lip and giving her a chance to gasp in air. Her fingers swept down his muscled stomach, and then further down to find his hard cock.

"Goddamn!" He spat out the word as though it'd tried to poison him. Silvia's fingers trailed further still over his balls and he pushed her down hard suddenly, trapping her hand against the flat of his stomach. The bulk of his body pinned her down and though he weighed maybe seventy pounds more than her, she didn't feel the weight but more of a pressing possessiveness, something shielding and almost sweet.

He shifted a little, his body arching up so he could press his cock between her legs. It made them both groan. Silvia had never had an intimate experience like the one transpiring. Ronan seemed desperately patient, as though some part of him wanted to make it last. Had she ever wanted anything so much? Her hips lifted searchingly, trying to feel his hardness, trying to figure out a way she could make it touch her enough to hurt.

His hands moved to her waist.

"You want to fuck?" His mouth touched the corner of hers, lips brushing her skin as he spoke. She could feel the clench of his jaw as she pushed against him.

"Please," she breathed. "*please*."

He pulled back a little and then he pushed her legs wider, bending one up to get better access. Silvia wanted to watch him but as the head of his cock pushed against her clit, she felt like she might pass out. Her eyes closed desperately, her hands pulling at his shoulders in an attempt to get him closer. Ronan's breath came out harshly and bar the beat of her own heart, she couldn't hear anything else. It took a few precious seconds for him to line up and then he pushed inside her, his hard cock disappearing into her dripping snatch. It felt like she'd been waiting for it her entire life.

"That's – so – good," she breathed unaware she'd said the words out loud until he responded.

"You got that right, Silver." His voice sounded low and heavy, strained with forced patience.

He fit inside her sublimely, stretching her in all the right ways and once he'd sunk in, she felt as though she could hold him there forever. For a few pulse-quickening seconds, a fear that he might finish too soon flooded her but then he pulled back, letting out a controlled breath.

"So – goddamn – *tight*," he growled and then nothing made sense anymore.

He fucked hard, driving into her over and over, getting impossibly deeper each time. It hurt in the best way. Silvia's hands scrabbled over his back, wanting to feel every last millimetre of his skin, to become accustomed with each muscular curve and unrelenting bone. She gasped with each brutal thrust, her body sweating and pushing beneath his. If she hadn't been so lost in him, she might have been embarrassed at her wantonness.

"You fuck so good," Ronan grunted. "So – so – *good*."

His fingers dug into her flesh, finding bone and trying to dig even deeper. It hurt but she reciprocated, nails clawing at his shoulders until he snarled. It felt like a fight, a race even, something competitive but mutual, something that made no sense but cried out as fundamentally essential. Nothing mattered more than meeting each of his punishing thrusts; than slamming her body back against his.

It became a blur, too fast, too urgent and the more she pushed up at him, the harder he pushed her back down until all of a sudden, something inside her gave and she pushed so hard and unexpectedly that he lost his balance and they fell off the sofa and onto the floor, her on top.

"I'm so sorry," Silvia gasped.

Ronan didn't speak. His hands gripped harder to her waist and he pushed her over easily, reclaiming his place on top.
"I'll survive," he growled and then resumed where they'd left off, his hips lifting and jolting her into the carpeted floor. Silvia did her best to try and keep the pace but soon enough she'd lost and had to content herself with taking the force of his driving cock.

He came without warning, the hard rhythm suddenly interrupted by a snarling groan as he jerked inside her, flooding her snatch with his come. Even then, he didn't stop thrusting, encouraging her to push back until she fell apart beneath him, her orgasm so intense that she cried out. They were breathing hard, almost dangerously so. Ronan moved to lie beside her on the floor and even then, it took a good few moments for anything but the pleasure to enter her mind.

Turning slightly, she looked at him and then looked again. He'd always looked flawlessly attractive when he'd strolled into the office. But now she looked at him naked, without the distraction of sex and saw him for the first time. His scars were ugly, deliberate imperfections ruining what would have been a flawless body. Bullet wounds, stab marks, the jagged remnants of lacerations. A new gash marred his upper arm, and it looked poorly stitched together.

"I had to do it with my left hand," he said, seeing her frown. "I'm still crap at it."

The same feeling that had made her want to hug him earlier came over her again, only this time she wanted to fix him. Soap and warm water and clean bandages. Maybe make him drink some alcohol. Something strong enough to let everything become warm and okay.

"Vitamin E oil is good for scars," She heard herself saying and almost immediately wanted to hide.

He didn't laugh at her. He smiled.

"I'll keep that in mind, Silver." His smile lingered and then disappeared. "Though you ought to know that cigarettes will probably kill you."

She'd never smoked in the office, always been careful to keep her occasional habit a prioritised secret. But he knew. He seemed to know everything. She wondered if he might even know about the small cash hoard under her bed.

"Stalker," she said, her voice light and deliberately playful.

The smile reappeared.

"I'm good at my job."

"I'm not your job," she countered.

"Not officially."

It made her smile, then made her think.

"How the hell did we get here?" she breathed, the question more of a thought.

It took a while for him to answer.

"I felt it coming the first day I saw you," he said, finally. "You know when you just know? That something has to give, something has to happen, there's too much tension, too much pressure? I feel it all the time but never in this way. It's usually when someone's trying to stab me in the back."

He looked at the ceiling.

"I mean, I trust everyone until they give me a reason not to. Most of them disappoint me."

"But?" Silvia unthinkingly supplied the word he held back. His head turned. "But you haven't. Ever. And that makes me feel hopeful that maybe life can be worth more than it ever has been. You know?"

Silvia smiled.

"Yeah. I know."

About the Author

Hannah Blackbird is a 23 year old writer of erotic and romantic fiction, with stories that have become firm favourites with men and women alike. Her stories like to delve deep into the personalities and inner thoughts of her characters in order to bring them to life.

A number of her erotic stories have won awards and are widely lauded amongst the erotic writing community. Hannah has been writing creatively since childhood and has always enjoyed reading; her favourite weekends are those spent getting lost in libraries. When she's not writing, Hannah can be found working in finance, browsing fashion websites, baking or people watching. She currently lives in the UK with her husband, and more books than her bookcases can take.

Good Story Great Erotica
From the Same Publisher
Hit and Run No Escape
by Jim Masters

It's a cold wet dark winter's evening and Jack is on his way home from work when he witnesses a young woman being knocked down by a hit and run driver in a white van.

He covers the girl to keep her dry and warm and calls 999. He accompanies the girl to hospital mainly to get his coat back. But he stays and she gains consciousness he takes her to his home to recover overnight.

They are immediately attracted to each other and some steamy hot erotic scenes play out. But who is the mysterious driver that tried to kill her!! Read this book and beg for more, just like Kirsty.

This is also read by the author as an audiobook. Listen whenever and wherever you want in private. On the train or in the car, on your work break or when you are just relaxing
VERY POPULAR ON AUDIBLE AND KINDLE

To keep up to date with the work of Jim Masters, promotions and free books sign up for his newsletter **www.jimmasters.co.uk**

Printed in Great Britain
by Amazon